나는 음식이다

아시아에서는 《바이링궐 에디션 한국 대표 소설》을 기획하여 한국의 우수한 문학을 주제별로 엄선해 국내외 독자들에게 소개합니다. 이 기획은 국내외 우수한 번역가들이 참여하여 원작의 품격을 최대한 살렸습니다. 문학을 통해 아시아의 정체성과 가치를 살피는 데 주력해 온 아시아는 한국인의 삶을 넓고 깊게 이해하는 데 이 기획이 기여하기를 기대합니다.

Asia Publishers presents some of the very best modern Korean literature to readers worldwide through its new Korean literature series 〈Bilingual Edition Modern Korean Literature〉. We are proud and happy to offer it in the most authoritative translation by renowned translators of Korean literature. We hope that this series helps to build solid bridges between citizens of the world and Koreans through a rich in-depth understanding of Korea.

바이링궐 에디션 한국 대표 소설 066
Bi-lingual Edition Modern Korean Literature 066

I Am Food

오수연
나는 음식이다

Oh Soo-yeon

ASIA
PUBLISHERS

Contents

나는 음식이다

I Am Food

누군가 문을 두드려. 머리맡에서 뭔가 부서진 것도 같고. 잠결에도 나는 이게 무슨 소리인지 알아챘어. 벽 속에서 낡은 수도관이 요동치고 있어. 새벽에 이웃에서 물을 틀면 수도관은 별별 소리를 다 내. 녹슨 기관차가 굴러가는 쇳소리를 낸 적도 있지. 밤새 굳어버린 뼈마디를 고통스럽게 움직이는 듯이, 오늘은 꼼짝도 못하겠다고 한바탕 버텨보려는 것처럼. 그래봤자 잉잉잉 울면서 물을 끌어올리는 하루의 노역을 시작하기 마련이야. 한밤중까지 울어.

콩콩콩 윗집에서 생강을 찧는군. 우유차를 끓이는 거야. 생강이야 기본이고, 그 밖에 차에 풍미를 더하기 위

Somebody's knocking on the door. Or something by my bed's been broken. Even half asleep, I recognize the sound. The ancient water pipe inside the wall is convulsing again. It makes all kinds of noise when neighbors turn the water on. Once I heard the metallic clanging of a rusted steam engine running. As if it were struggling to move its joints that had stiffened up overnight, as if to say it wouldn't budge, digging in its heels. Still, it's bound to end up whimpering, and begin a day's labor of hauling up water. And it continues whimpering into the night.

Thump thump thump! They're pounding ginger up-

해 넣는 향신료는 집집마다 달라. '일라찌'는 한두 알만 떨궈도 집 근처가 다 들큰해져. 골목을 지나가던 행인이 어느 집에서 맛있는 차를 끓이나 하고 두리번거려. 계피를 툭툭 분질러 넣는 집이 있는가 하면, 창틀에 박하 화분을 기르면서 차 끓일 때마다 몇 잎 훑어 넣는 집도 있고. 향이 우러나도록 찻잎과 향신료를 충분히 끓인 다음 설탕을 듬뿍 치고, 차 한 잔 분량에 한 국자씩 우유를 떠 넣는 거야. 막 끓인 차 내음을 맡으면 누구라도 목이 말라지지. 나는 침대에 누운 채로 마른침을 삼켰어. 공기가 차서 코끝이 찡해.

연기가 방에 차고 있어. 아랫집에서 기름을 많이 붓고 식빵을 굽나봐. 그 집 부엌에서 뭔가를 구울 때마다 연기가 하수도관을 타고 우리집까지 올라와. 차 향내에 빵 굽는 냄새까지 섞여 내 방에 거하게 아침상이라도 봐놓은 것 같아. 담요를 당겨 얼굴을 덮어보지만 거기에도 냄새가 배어 있어. 숨을 들이쉴 때마다 가루비누 향 대신 고소한 기름내가 나는군. 옆집에서 찻잔을 달그락거려. 모래가 부슬거리도록 벽이 물러서 이웃집에서 나는 소리들이 고스란히 들려. 인사를 나눈 적도 없는데 나는 옆집 식구들의 행동거지를 같이 살아본 것처

stairs to boil milk tea. Ginger is a given, and each home puts in different spices to add to the flavor of the tea. Just a seed or two of "elaichi" can fill a home's surroundings with a sweet-savory aroma. Passersby in the alley will look around in search of the home with the delicious tea brewing. Some households break a couple of cinnamon sticks and put them in, while others strip a few mint leaves from potted plants by the windows. When the water has been boiling long enough to draw out the flavor from the tealeaves and spices, you add a generous serving of sugar, and then dole out a ladleful of milk for each cup of tea. Anyone will get thirsty with a whiff of that just-brewed tea smell. I swallow hard while lying in bed. My nose tingles from the cold air.

Smoke is filling up the room. They must be baking bread downstairs with lots of oil. Whenever that home bakes something, the smoke comes up to my place through the sewage pipe. Based on the aroma of tea mixed with the smell of baked bread, it feels as though there should be an extravagant breakfast waiting in my room. I pull my blanket up over my face, but the blanket is also soaked with the smells. With every breath I take, there is the

럼 속속들이 알아. 아까부터 아줌마가 아이들을 깨우느라고 애를 먹고 있어.

나는 돌아누워 얼굴을 베개에 묻었어. 구웠다기보다는 튀겨냈다고나 해야 할 아랫집의 식빵이 너무나 먹고 싶어. 원래 빵을 좋아하는 편은 아닌데 지금은 그걸 못 먹으면 미칠 것만 같아. 두 달도 넘게 흰죽만 먹고 있으니 속이 헛헛해서 허리가 접힐 지경이야. 눈과 코와 입은 극도로 예민해졌지. 길거리에서 눈에 들어오느니 음식점 간판뿐이요, 사람하고 마주 앉으면 그가 몇 시간 전에 점심으로 뭘 먹었는지부터 냄새로 감지하게 되는 거야. 어쩌다 뭐라도 입에 넣으면 혀가 맛을 본다기보다는 빨아들이는 것 같아.

그러나 숟가락을 놓고 돌아서는 즉시 골치가 띵하고 먹은 게 후회가 돼. 그리고 기다렸다는 듯이 격렬한 위통이 일지. 하물며 맛있는 거 먹는 상상만 해도 이 뿌리가 뻐근하도록 군침은 도는데, 바로 그 순간 위가 면도날로 그어지는 것처럼 아릿한 거야. 지금도 식빵이 먹고 싶다는 생각이 들자마자 속이 쓰리기 시작했어. 식욕에 대해 응징이라도 하는 듯이 위통이 뒤따르고, 그 위통에 대해 반발이라도 하는 것처럼 식욕은 더욱더 강

delicious smell of grease instead of a scent of detergent. Teacups are clattering next door. The walls are soft to the point where they almost crumble into sand. I can hear every single noise my neighbors make. Although I have never even said hello to them, like someone who's lived with them I know each and every move of theirs. The woman has, for example, been having a hard time trying to wake her kids up.

I roll over and bury my face in the pillow. I am dying to eat the downstairs neighbors' bread, the bread more fried than toasted. Usually not a big fan of bread, at this moment I think I might go nuts if I don't eat it. I feel so empty inside from over two months of eating only white rice porridge that my body is about to fold over. My eyes, nose and mouth have become ultra-sensitive. I can only see restaurant signs on the streets, and I can tell by the smell what someone has had for lunch a few hours ago when I sit across the table from them. On the rare occasion I get to put something in my mouth, I seem to vacuum it up before my tongue even touches it.

But the instant I put my spoon down and turn around, my head aches and I regret eating. Then,

해져. 이런 것도 단지 위장병이라고 할 수밖에 없나. 그런 평범한 이름을 붙이기가 나로서는 억울해. 증상이 너무 악랄해. 뭔가 끔찍한 명칭이 따로 있어야 할 것 같아. 이를테면…… 괴질, 현대 의학의 수수께끼, 신이 내린 천벌!

만나는 사람들마다 걱정을 해준다고 위장병에는 어떤 음식이 좋고 뭐는 나쁘다는 얘기를 하지. 그 말이 다 달라. 내가 알기로는 위에 탈이 났을 때는 쌀죽이 가장 낫고 밀가루 음식, 유제품, 생야채나 과일은 안 좋다고 했어. 여기 사람들은 정반대야. 자기들이 늘상 먹는, 발효시키지 않고 구운 빵하고 콩이 소화가 가장 잘 된대. 나보고 쌀로 지은 밥이나 죽은 절대로 먹지 말라는 거야. 어떤 영국 여자는 세끼 다 야채샐러드만 먹어보라고 했어. 반면에 설령 위가 건강하다고 해도 야채는 익혀 먹어야 한다는 중국인도, 레몬과 오렌지를 먹지 말라는 티베트 사람도 있었지.

뭐가 좋다더라는 얘기야 그런가보다 하고 넘길 수 있지만 뭘 먹으면 안 된다는 말은 한번 들으면 잊혀지지가 않아. 어떤 음식이건 긍정적인 면도 있을 텐데 내가 기억하는 건 그게 어째서 안 좋다는 귀띔뿐이야. 뭐는

as if on cue, I get severe stomach pain. Just picturing eating something delicious will give me a sensation of a razor blade running over my stomach, even as my teeth drown from the water in my mouth. This time, too, my stomach starts to burn the second I feel like eating the bread. The stomach pain follows, almost like punishment for my appetite, and in turn my appetite becomes stronger then as if rebelling against the stomach pain. Is this still just a type of stomach problem? It doesn't seem fair to me to give it such an ordinary name. My symptoms are too vicious. It feels as though there should be a separate, horrific name for it. Like... a strange malady, a mystery of modern medicine, or divine punishment!

Well-meaning people tell me what kinds of food are good, and bad, for stomach problems. No two say the same thing. My understanding was that rice porridge was best for fixing a malfunctioning stomach, and wheat products, dairy, raw vegetables and fruits were bad. People here say the opposite. They say bread baked without yeast and beans, what they eat all the time, are the easiest to digest. So I should never eat cooked rice or porridge made with rice. A British woman told me to

이래서 안 되고 다른 건 저래서 안 좋고, 이건 피해야 하고 저것도 삼가야 하며, 멀리해야 하고, 꺼릴 이유가 있고, 참아야 할 필요가 있으며 되도록 먹지 않는 게 낫고, 안 된다, 안 된다, 안 된다……

결국 아무것도 먹지 않는 도리밖에는 없는지도 몰라. 음식을 보지도, 가까이 하지도, 먹는 데 대해 생각하지도 말아야 할 거야. 그러면 식욕을 안 느낄 테고 식욕이 없으면 뒤따르는 위통도 생길 수가 없겠지. 그래야 비로소 이걸 먹어도 되나 안 되나, 몸에 해로운가 아닌가 하는 중단 없는 고민으로부터 놓여날 수 있을 거야. 아마 내 위장병을 고치는 유일한 처방은 그것뿐일 거야. 안 먹고 사는 것.

발로 침대 밑을 휘저어 슬리퍼를 찾아 꿰고 나는 일어났어. 몇 걸음 걷다가 멈춰 섰지. 침대에서 왜 나왔는지를 모르겠어. 앞집에 가려진 창문 한 귀퉁이로 하늘이 겨우 보여. 까마귀 떼가 맴을 돌고 있어. 뒤얽힌 골목 어디선가 시커먼 연기가 피어올라. 누군가 몸을 녹이려고 쓰레기를 태우고 있을 테지. 얼음이 얼기엔 턱도 없는 추위지만 열대에서 겨울은 난감한 계절이야. 여름만

have only a vegetable salad for every meal. Then there was a Chinese person who insisted that even those with healthy stomachs should cook all their vegetables. And a Tibetan told me to stay away from lemons and oranges.

Advice on what's good to eat may get a ho-hum reaction from me, but I can never forget a thing on any don't-eat list. I mean there must be a beneficial effect to any food, yet all I remember are tips on how certain foods are bad for you. Something is a no-no for this reason, and something else is bad for that reason; this is to be avoided and that is to be skipped, to be kept at bay. This is why you should dislike this, why you need to refrain from that; you shouldn't eat this if you can help it, no, no, and no...

Ultimately, perhaps the only option left is not to eat anything. I should not see, keep close to, or think about eating food. Then I wouldn't have an appetite, and with no appetite I wouldn't have the stomach pains that follow. Only then would I be freed from the unceasing dilemma of trying to discern if I could eat something, if something was bad for my body. That's probably the only prescription for curing my stomach problem: live without eating.

생각하고 지은 집들은 난방시설이 없고 설령 전기난로를 켠다 해도 온기를 가두지 못해. 그런 집이나마 없는 떠돌이들에게는 영상 10도라 해도 치명적이지. 조간신문에 실리는, 간밤에 얼어 죽은 동사자들의 숫자가 날마다 늘어나. 바짝 추웠던 건 두어 달쯤인데 나는 몇 달은 고생한 느낌이야. 아니 반년, 혹은 몇 년 동안이나 이렇게 몸을 웅숭그리고 지냈던 것만 같아. 허리를 쭉 펴고 산 기억이 아득해. 달고 뜨거운 차…… 뜨거운…… 국물!

표고버섯 때문이야. 어느새 나는 점심 메뉴를 걱정하고 있었던 거야. 침대에서 벌떡 일어난 건 건버섯을 담가놓아야 한다는 생각이 들어서였어. 미지근한 물에 담근다 해도 마른 표고를 불리려면 두 시간은 걸려. 탁상시계를 보니 일곱 시가 채 안 됐어. 다모가 오기로 한 열두 시까지 다섯 시간이나 남았지. 그러나 방금 전에도 시간은 충분하다는 생각을 했건만 나도 모르게 부엌으로 가고 있었듯이, 이미 나는 정신이 온통 요리에 쏠려 있어. 까닭 없이 숨이 가쁘고 심장이 쿵덕거려. 입술까지 바짝 말랐어. 쫓기는 사람처럼.

뭘 먹고, 어떻게 해 먹을까 하는 고민으로 내 머리는

Fishing under the bed, my feet find their way into my slippers, and I get up. I stop after a few steps. I forget why I got out of bed. I can see a small piece of the sky through a corner of the window that is mostly blocked by the house next door. Crows are circling. Black smoke is rising from somewhere in the labyrinth of alleys. Someone must be burning trash in order to get warm. Though this cold never comes close to forming ice, you're at a loss for what to do with winters in the tropics. Houses built with only summer in mind do not come with heating systems, and there is no way to retain warmth from electric heaters, if you have them. And for those drifters without shelter, ill-equipped for the cold, even a 50-degree weather can be fatal. Every day, morning papers list more people who have frozen to death overnight. Although we've only had a real cold spell for a couple of months, it feels like at least several months to me. No, half a year, if not a few years, is how long I feel I've spent hunched up like this. I can't remember the last time I straightened my back. Sweet, hot tea ...Hot soup!

Oh, it was the shitake mushrooms. I was already worrying about the lunch menu. I sprang out of my bed because I figured I had to put dried mush-

터져버릴 것 같아. 밤마다 돌아눕고 또 돌아누우며 야채 요리법을 궁리하지. 양념을 적게 쓰면서도 풋내 안 나게, 또 단조롭지도 않게 채소를 익히는 방법은? 생채도, 묵힌 김치류도 안 되고, 날것이 아니면서 신선해야 하는데. 꿈속에서는 채식주의자를 위한 식단이 보여. 공항의 전광판처럼 칸마다 내용들이 분주히 바뀌고 있어.

감기가 영 낫지를 않는대. 저번 주에 그랬듯이 오늘도 다모는 목에 손수건을 친친 감고 왔어. 침을 삼키기도 괴롭다며 묻는 말에 대답 없이 인상만 써. 식탁에 앉아서도 그는 먹을 생각을 안 해. 음식에서 김이 다 나가도록 바라만 보고 있는 거야. 그가 그러고 있는 시간이 길어질수록 나는 점점 더 불안해. 뭐가 잘못 들어갔나, 보기 좋으라고 뿌린 깨소금에서 묵은 냄새가 나나, 갖은 생각이 스쳐가. 사람이 말이야 상을 받았으면 먹고 싶지 않아도 음식을 입에 대는 체는 해주는 게 예의가 아니겠어. 제발 그가 볼이 미어지게 입에 우겨 넣고 쩝쩝거리며 먹어주었으면 좋겠어. 한 번만이라도 그래준다면 내 속이 다 후련할 거 같아. 다모에게 왕성한 식욕을 내려달라고 하늘에 기도라도 하고 싶어. 요리접시를 노

rooms in water. Even in lukewarm water, it takes dried shitake a couple of hours to soak. I look at the clock on the table to see that it is a few minutes to seven. I have as long as five hours till noon, when Damo is supposed to come. Yet I find myself automatically walking over to the kitchen, despite thinking there is enough time. And now I'm totally focused on cooking. My breath is short for no reason, and my heart beats loudly. Even my lips are dry. Like someone on the run.

My head feels like exploding from worrying about what to eat and how to prepare it. Every night, I keep rolling and turning in bed, trying to think up ways to cook vegetables. How to use spices sparingly while getting rid of the unripe taste, or how to cook vegetables so they aren't monotonous. They can be neither uncooked nor fermented like *kimchi*, and they have to be fresh without being raw. I see a menu for vegetarians in my dreams. Its rows are busy flicking and changing like the arrival and departure board at an airport.

The cold isn't going away, he says. Like last week, he's come with his neck wrapped with a handkerchief. He says it even hurts to swallow,

려보고 있는 그가 무서워.

나도 침통하게 내 몫의 흰죽 사발이나 내려다보고 있을 수밖에. 그런데 눈이 마주칠까봐 겁이 나면서도 자꾸 다모를 힐끔거리게 돼. 감기 때문에 안색이 더욱 나빠진 그의 얼굴에 여드름인지 열꽃인지 뾰루지가 산만하게 불거져 있어. 목을 저토록 조여놓아 피가 머리로 몰린 탓인지 뾰루지들은 발그족족하게 독이 올랐어. 가슴속에서 뭔가 북받쳐 오르는데 그게 자칫 웃음일까봐 나는 어금니를 깨물었어. 이 와중에도 위통은 쑤셨다가 아렸다가, 옆으로 옮겨가는 척하다가 얼른 제자리로 돌아오기도 하면서 따로 살아 있는 듯이 생생해.

마침내 긴 한숨과 함께 그는 숟가락을 들었어. 그걸 공기밥의 소복한 꼭대기에 푹 꽂더니 밥을 절반 이상이나 접시에 덜어내는 거야. 그러고는 접시를 가장자리까지 밀어내며 속삭였어.

"너무……"

정말 다모는 목이 많이 쉬었군. 현관을 들어서며 마지못해 내게 한마디 '하이!' 했던 이후 반 시간 새 병세가 더 나빠진 것 같아. 그의 말소리를 나는 거의 알아들을 수가 없어.

making faces in place of replies. He's seated at the table, but shows no interest in eating. He's gazing at the food while all its steam rises. The longer he stares like this, the more anxious I get. Did something wrong get in? Do the sesame seeds, which I sprinkled as a visual garnish, smell stale? My mind races. If someone has prepared a table for you, isn't it common manners to pretend to bring the food to your mouth at least, even if you don't feel like eating it? I so would like for him to stuff his cheeks with food and chomp down. If he did that even once, I could exhale with relief. I feel like praying to the heavens to bestow on Damo a voracious appetite. It scares me to see him stare at the plates.

I can only look down miserably at the bowl of white rice porridge in front of me. Still, even as I fear catching his stare, I keep glancing over at Damo. His face, even more devoid of color from the cold, is covered with unruly blemishes, from acne or heat rash. And maybe because binding his neck has so tightly forced the blood to his head, the blemishes are raging, red and raw. I feel something coming up from my chest, and I have to clench my teeth because I'm afraid it may be a laugh. All the while, the pain in my stomach is alive

"네?"

"너무 많, 다, 구, 요."

더욱 작은 목소리로 되뇌고는 다모는 또 한숨을 쉬었어. 그리고 숟가락을 내려놓고 젓가락으로 밥알 두어 알갱이를 집어 입에 넣었어. 잊을 만하면 한 번씩 힘겹게 입을 우물거리는 모습이 보기에 안쓰러워. 그가 밥알을 삼키기 전에는 다시 한 번의 긴 한숨과 함께 몇 초 가량의 휴지기마저 있어.

다모는 오늘도 그냥 넘어가주지 않으려는 게 분명해. 입을 단단히 오므린 얼굴에 그렇게 씌어 있어. 매사에 원리원칙을 고수하는 그의 깔깔한 성미야 오늘 새삼스러운 것도 아니지만, 마주 앉아 감당하기에는 오늘도 여전히 충격적이야. 그가 숟가락으로 밥을 푹 쑤셨을 때 나는 명치에 뜨끔하는 고통마저 느꼈어. 내 가슴속에서도 무언가 밥무더기처럼 허물어져버렸어.

그래, 내 잘못이야. 내가 보기에도 그릇마다 너무 수북해. 접시들이 넓적해서인지 오늘따라 음식이 특히 많아 보이는 것 같아. 다모는 음식을 보면 그것이 상 위에 오르기 직전까지는 살아 있는 생명체였다는 생각이 제일 먼저 든대. 음식을 낭비하는 행위는 생물을 학살하

and well, as if it had a life of its own, piercing one minute then grating the next, seemingly moving to my side only to come back to its original spot in no time.

Finally he picks up his spoon with a long sigh. He sticks it down into the center of his full bowl of rice, and then doles out more than half of the rice onto a plate. Then, pushing the plate all the way to the edge of the table, he whispers.

"It's too..."

Wow, Damo is really hoarse. His condition has apparently worsened in the half hour since he begrudgingly uttered "Hi!" to me as he came through the door. I can hardly make out what he says.

"I'm sorry?"

"It. Is. Too. Much."

Damo recites in a voice softer still, and follows with another sigh. He puts down the spoon and then uses chopsticks to pick up a couple of grains of rice to put into his mouth. It breaks my heart to see him move his mouth painstakingly every once in a while almost as an afterthought. There's even a pause lasting several seconds accompanied by another long sigh before he swallows the rice.

It's obvious Damo will not go easy on me today,

는 거나 마찬가지라고 그는 밥 먹을 때마다 말하지. 번번이 터무니없이 많은 음식을 만들어버리는 내 손에 피라도 묻어 있는 양 끔찍하게 쳐다봐.

하지만 나는 요리만 할라치면 해놓고 나서 혹시 모자라면 어쩌나 하는 걱정이 앞서는걸. 쌀 한 컵이면 되는 줄 알면서 모자라는 것보다야 남는 게 낫다는 생각에 한 컵 더 푸고, 쌀통 뚜껑 닫다 말고 얼른 반 컵을 더 퍼. 그게 나쁜 습관이란 건 나도 알아. 예전엔 나도 안 그랬어. 위장병을 얻고 난 뒤로 이 괴상한 버릇이 생겼어.

미역무침을 한 젓가락 집으며 그가 묻는 듯한 시선을 던졌어. 웬 고춧가루가 들어 있느냐는 뜻이지. 다모는 마늘, 파, 고춧가루 같은 매운 양념을 싫어해. 그런 걸 먹으면 위가 나빠질 뿐만 아니라 성격이 화를 잘 내는 다혈질로 변한대.

"색깔을 내느라고 고춧가루를 요만큼만 썼어요."

나는 손가락 한 마디를 짚어 보였어. 그의 눈길이 내 손에 와 닿는 순간 마디를 짚은 손톱이 저절로 밀려 올라갔지. 지레 주눅이 들어 나도 모르게 손마디에 표시된 면적을, 즉 미역무침에 들어간 고춧가루의 양을 줄였던 거야. 그래봤자 소용도 없이 다모의 표정은 심각

either. It says so on his face, on his tightly pursed lips. It's nothing new, his finicky nature, sticking to his principles in all things. Yet it is still hard for me to bear it, seated across from him. When he poked deep into the rice with his spoon, I even felt a sharp pain at the pit of my stomach. In my heart, too, something crumbled like that mound of rice.

Yes, it's my fault. Even I can see that the dishes are overloaded. Maybe because the plates are square, it appears that there is a lot of food, particularly today. When he sees food, Damo says, the first thing that comes into his mind is that it was a living creature up until the very moment it came on the table. His favorite saying whenever he has a meal is that wasting food is exactly like slaughtering living beings. He routinely looks at my hands in horror as if there were blood on them from making exorbitant amounts of food.

But above all else, what concerns me when I'm set to cook is if there will be enough when I'm done cooking. Knowing full well that a cup of rice will do, I scoop one more, thinking it's better to have leftovers than not enough, and I go for another quick half cup after closing the canister halfway. I know it's a terrible habit. I wasn't like that

해지기만 했어. 야채볶음 한 젓가락을 맛본 후에는 두 배로 더 심각해졌고. 그는 된장찌개는 아예 쳐다보지도 않아. 세 번째로 밥알을 입에 넣고 반찬을 먹을 차례가 되었을 때는 도무지 먹을 만한 게 없다는 듯이 젓가락을 든 채로 식탁을 빙 둘러보았어. 그러더니 자기가 전번에 갖다준 김을 서너 장 집어 밥 위에 올려놓고 고개를 숙여버렸어. 그것만 먹을 작정인가봐.

이럴 줄 몰랐나 뭐, 원래 이런 사람인걸, 관두라고 그래! 상처받지 않으려고 나는 진작부터 이 세 마디를 주문처럼 외우고 있어. 그런데 별 효과가 없어. 얼굴이 확확 달아올라.

"왜요? 어디 아파요? 뭐 잘못된 거라도 있어요?"

다모가 쥐어짜는 목소리로 물었어. 나는 고개를 저었어. 그러나 손대는 이 없이 남아 있는 음식들이야말로 뭔가 잘못돼도 한참 잘못됐다는 증거가 아니겠어. 나는 먹을 수가 없고 그는 먹기가 싫대. 밥알을 깨작대는 그와 흰죽을 헤적거리는 나 사이에서 가엾은 반찬들만 식어가고 있어.

"이거요……"

그가 젓가락으로 뭔가를 집어내 내 코앞에 들이댔어.

before. I only developed this odd habit after I got my stomach problem.

Picking up the sautéed wakame seaweed with his chopsticks, he shoots me an interrogative look. He wants to know why there is ground chili pepper in it. Damo hates strong spices like garlic, scallion and chili pepper. He says eating those will not only damage your stomach but also turn you into someone hot-blooded and quick to anger.

"I used just this much chili pepper," I touch the underside of the top joint of my index finger with the tip of my thumb. "For color."

The instant I feel his look on my hand, my thumb automatically slides up toward the tip of the finger. I've caved in again, reducing the area on my finger indicating the amount of ground chili pepper in the sautéed seaweed. It's all in vain, though, as Damo looks even more serious now. A taste of the stir-fried vegetables doubles the seriousness. He's not even looking at the miso stew. After he puts grains of rice into his mouth for the third time and it's time for a side dish, he surveys the table while holding the chopsticks as if to say there is nothing worth eating on it. Then he picks up a few pieces of dried laver, which he brought me last time, lays

야채볶음에서 골라낸 호박쪼가리야. 드디어 그가 말문을 열었어. 풀 죽은 내 꼴이 보기 안돼서 분위기를 바꿔보려는 거지. 이미 속이야 상할 대로 상했지만 그가 성의를 보인다면야 나도 보조는 맞춰줘야겠지. 나는 꺼멍게 죽어가던 희망의 불꽃을 간신히 되살렸어. 이제부터라도 시작해보자는 말이지? 행복한 식사 시간.

"반가워서 한번 사봤어요. 여기에도 이런 호박이 있는 줄은 몰랐거든요. 우리 고향에서는……"

수줍게 나는 말문을 열었어. 병 때문에 낯빛이 어두울 뿐인 그를 나 혼자 괜히 미워해서 미안해.

"호박? 이건 오이라구요. 오이의 일종. 이걸 이렇게 만드는 사람은 난 오늘 처음 봤어요."

"오……이!"

마음속 희망의 불꽃을 나는 황급히 눌러 껐어. 아까 이 애호박 비슷한 걸 썰면서 어쩐지 껍질이 너무 두껍다 싶긴 했지.

"내 생각에는요, 아무 재료나 이것저것 뒤섞어서 잡동사니를 만들어버리는 건 좋은 요리법이 아닌 것 같아요."

"……"

them on top of the rice, and puts his head down. Apparently, that is all he is eating.

Well, like I didn't know he'd do this. This is just who he is. Fine, he can just leave it, then! For a while, I repeat to myself these three phrases like a spell, so I won't get hurt. But they're not working. My face burns.

"What is it? Are you sick? Is something wrong?"

Damo's voice is strained. I shake my head. But what clearer evidence than these dishes of food, touched by no one, do you need that something is awfully wrong? I can't eat, and he won't eat. These poor side dishes are getting cold between his picking at his rice and my stirring at my white rice porridge.

"Here..."

He picks something out with his chopsticks to shove in front of my nose. It's a piece of zucchini from the vegetable stir-fry. He has finally begun to talk. He's trying to change the atmosphere because he feels bad seeing me so crushed. Though already upset, I ought to respond in kind to his show of consideration. I manage to revive the flame of hope was flickering out. So you want to start over now, right? A happy lunch.

나도 내가 요리를 잘한다고는 생각하지 않아. 씹히는 맛이 있도록 호박, 아니 오이를 센 불에 얼른 볶아내려고 했는데 해놓고 보니 미끈거렸어. 게다가 곁들인 표고버섯의 물이 들어 거무튀튀하기까지 한 거야. 검은 빛깔이나 제대로 내려고 간장을 붓고, 너무 볼품없는 것 같아 배추를 좀 썰어 넣었지. 식단에 있던 배추된장국 대신 임기응변으로 된장찌개를 끓였고. 부엌에 들어가기를 죽기보다 싫어했던 나로서는 그야말로 죽어서 새로 태어났다는 각오로 요리에 임했던 거야. 고기와 생선, 조개류, 달걀 같은 동물성 식품을 일절 피하고, 우유와 유제품마저 안 쓰고, 양념도 안 넣고, 화학조미료도 안 치고, 그러면서 짜지도 달지도 않게 음식을 하기가 어디 쉬운가.

"이걸로 국을 끓이면 얼마나 근사한데요. 다른 건 아무것도 필요 없이 물만 붓고 소금만 아주 약간 치면 되는데. 나한테 미리 물어볼 수도 있었잖아요."

"……"

몰랐다고, 호박이건 오이건 다음번엔 꼭 국을 끓이겠노라고 대답하려는데 입이 안 떨어져. 입을 열었다가 그 말이 아니라 생뚱맞은 말이 튀어나오면 어떻게 해.

"Oh, I was glad to find those. I didn't know they had that kind of zucchinis here. Back home, we—"

Shyly, I open my mouth. I'm sorry for griping about him for no reason, when he just looks that way because of his sickness.

"Zucchini? This is a cucumber. A type of cucumber. I've never seen anyone cook a cucumber like this."

"Cuke...umber!"

I rush to stamp out the flames of hope in my heart. I did think it odd when I was cutting this baby cucumber-like thing with its thick skin.

"If you ask me, I don't think it's a good recipe to mix any and all ingredients together and make this hodgepodge."

I never said I was a good cook. I meant to fry the zucchini—no, the cucumber, over high heat quickly so that it would still be crunchy. When I was done, it was slimy. Plus, it looked all blackish from the shitake I'd cooked with it. I decided to add soy sauce to accentuate the black color, then tossed in some chopped cabbage to spruce it up. And in place of the miso soup with cabbage that was on the menu, I improvised with a miso stew. I was utterly committed to cooking like someone reborn; I

뭔가, 해서는 안 될 말. 그런데 다모가 돌연 새침해졌어. 내 입술은 가만히 있었는데 눈이나 뺨이나, 다른 것들이 움직였나봐.

"알았어요, 알았다니까요. 난 이제부터 아무 말 안 할 테니까 당신 맘대로 해요. 어차피 내 일도 아닌데 내가 왜 참견했는지 모르겠어요. 미안해요. 내가 한마디라도 충고할 때마다 당신은 날 당장 죽일 것처럼 보여요."

"당신이야말로 내가 무슨 음식을 내놓든 자살할 것처럼 보인다구요."

속에 있던 말을 막상 해놓고 보니 노엽다기보다는 서러워. 목소리가 심히 떨려. 아까부터 가슴속에서 복받쳐 오르던 건 웃음이 아니라 울음이었나봐.

"아, 물론 당신이 요리하느라 애썼다는 거 알아요. 정말 고맙게 생각한다니까요. 하지만 의사가 나보고 감자를 먹지 말라고 하는데 어떻게 해요. 감기가 영 안 떨어져서 며칠 전에 한의사한테 가봤더니 나더러 앞으로 두 달간은 특히 음식을 조심하라고 하더라구요."

그게 바로 그가 된장찌개에 손도 안 댄 이유였어. 거기에 감자가 들어있거든.

"내가 만든 음식들은 죄다 당신한테 해롭지요."

used to hate stepping into the kitchen more than death itself. Do you think it's easy to avoid absolutely any animal products like beef, fish, seafood or eggs, to stay away from milk and any other kinds of dairy, and not touch spices or artificial seasonings, all the while making food that's neither salty nor sweet?

"It's wonderful to make soup with, you know. You don't need anything else—just put it in water with just a pinch of salt. You could have asked me beforehand, right?"

I try to reply that I didn't know, and that I will surely make soup with the zuke or cuke or whatever, but my mouth won't open. What if I open it and some nonsense comes out instead? Something I shouldn't say? But Damo has suddenly become standoffish anyway. Although my lips didn't move, I guess my eyes, cheeks, or some other parts of my face did instead.

"OK, fine, OK? I am not going to say anything from now on, so you can do whatever you want. It' s none of my business anyway, so I don't know why I even bothered. I'm sorry. Whenever I offer you a word of advice, you look like you're about to kill me."

"참내, 미안하다니까요. 그래도 좀 이해해줄 수 없어요? 요즘 내 몸이 정상이 아니잖아요. 감기 때문에 위가 더 나빠져서 아무거나 함부로 먹을 수가 없단 말이에요. 나중에 무슨 고생을 하든 일단 당신이 만들어놓은 건 내가 다 먹어야 한단 말인가요? 찹쌀은 쌀 중에서 가장 소화가 안 된다구요."

"찹쌀? 지금 찹쌀이라고 했어요? 무슨 소리예요? 찹쌀이 위에 좋다고 해서 여기서는 구하기도 어려운 걸 특별히……"

"누가 그래요? 위에 좋은 건 찹쌀죽이지 찹쌀밥이 아니에요. 보통 때 같으면 나도 상관 안 해요. 그렇지만 지금은 목이 아파서 이 자극적인 음식들을 도저히 삼킬 수가 없는 걸 어떻게 해요."

"매운 맛은 생강이에요. 마늘이나 고춧가루 때문이 아니라구요. 감기에는 생강이 약인 거 몰라요? 목이 아프다길래 내가 일부러 음식에 생강을 많이 넣었다구요."

"글쎄 누가 그러느냐구요. 암만 약이라도 정도가 있어야죠. 생강도 꿀하고 조화를 이뤄야 한다구요. 뭐든 맛이 지나치게 강하면 안 좋다고 내가 몇 번이나 얘기했는데. 당신은 내 말을 절대로 귀담아 듣지 않아요. 화내

"It's you who looks like you're about to kill yourself no matter what I put on the table."

Now that I've gotten everything off of my chest that's been inside of me I'm sad, oddly, rather than enraged. My voice is shaking terribly. I guess what's been coming up from my chest for a while wasn't a laugh but a sob.

"Oh. I know you really did your best here. I'm thankful for it, truly. But the doctor says not to eat potatoes, so what can I do? I saw a doctor of Eastern medicine a few days back because my cold wouldn't get better, and I was told to be extra careful with food the next couple of months."

That was why he didn't even touched the miso stew. It has potatoes.

"Every single dish of food I make is harmful for you."

"Come on, I said I'm sorry. Can't you be a little more understanding, though? You know my body isn't normal these days. My stomach is worse from the cold, so I can't go around eating just anything. Or are you saying I have to eat whatever you've made for me, no matter how much pain I might be in later? For digestion, sticky rice is the worst among all kinds of rice."

지 마세요. 고맙다고 했잖아요. 그래도 그렇지, 내가 보름도 넘게 죽도 못 넘기고 고생하는 줄 뻔히 알면서……"

"흑!"

급기야 나는 숟가락을 식탁에 내동댕이쳤어. 그리고 부엌을 뛰쳐나왔어.

"또, 또! 자꾸 왜 이러는 거예요? 이제부턴 내가 절대로 아무 말 안 하겠다고 그랬잖아요. 먹고 죽을지언정 한마디도 안 한다구요! 이 남은 음식들을 도대체 어쩔 거예요? 사람이 아무리 화가 나도 그렇지 난폭하게……"

나는 방문을 닫아걸고 침대에 몸을 던졌어. 머리카락을 쥐어뜯으며 울기 시작했어.

새벽에 속이 비었을 때, 매 끼니 30분 후에, 끼니 사이에 두 시간 간격으로, 잠자리에 들기 전에, 이렇게 일곱 여덟 번씩이나 약을 챙겨 먹다보면 어느새 하루가 다 가. 약을 먹기 위해 사는 것 같아. 그래봤자 병에 별 차도가 있는 것도 아니야. 내가 고향을 떠날 때 어머니는 모든 걸 시간이 해결해줄 거라고 말했지. 세상은 돌고

"Sticky rice? Did you say sticky rice? What are you talking about? I heard sticky rice is good for the stomach. So although it's really hard to get here, I especially—"

"Says who? Sticky rice porridge is good for the stomach, not steamed sticky rice. Normally I wouldn' t care. But now my throat hurts so much that I can't swallow these sharp-tasting things at all."

"The hot taste is the ginger. It's not from garlic or ground pepper. Don't you know ginger is a remedy for the cold? I used a lot of it intentionally because you told me you had a sore throat."

"Says who, I ask you? Even for drugs there should be some kind of limit. The ginger has to in balance with the honey. I've said time after time how nothing is good if there is too much taste from it, but you never heed my word. Don't get mad. I said thank you. Still, when you know all too well that I've suffered for over two weeks now... not even being able to keep porridge down—"

"Awk!"

Finally, I throw my spoon down on the table and run out of the kitchen.

"There you go again! Why do you keep doing this? Didn't I promise I wouldn't say anything ever

도는 법, 내가 받기만 하고 갚지 못한 은혜는 꼭 그 사람이 아니라 다른 누구한테 베풀면 되고, 혹시 마음에 쌓인 억울함이 있거들랑 다른 어느 누구한테 저지른 잘못을 대신 갚은 셈 치라는 거야. 하지만 생각해볼수록 나는 그 말이 위로 같지가 않아. 차라리 그 말은 어떤 식으로든 응분의 대가를 치르게 되리라는 경고가 아니었을까. 나를 원망하는 사람은 없다는데도 나는 위장병 때문에 하루도 편할 날이 없는걸. 시간이 해결해준다고? 겨울이 다 갔다지만 봄기운은 전혀 돌지 않잖아.

비계가 살보다 많은 고깃덩이는 살짝 들어 올려도 제풀에 낭창거려. 가느다란 뼈다귀에서 살집이 축 늘어졌을 때 똑, 제 반동으로 오므라들었을 때 똑, 두 방울의 소스가 식탁보에 찍혔어. 무라뜨는 손가락 끝으로 그걸 재빨리 훑어 입에 넣고는 쪽 빨았어. 그리고 막 떨어 지려는 세 번째 방울을 혀로 받치면서 덥석 고깃덩어리를 물었어. 잠시 고깃덩이와 그의 이빨 사이에 긴장이 인다 싶었는데 싱겁게도 살집 전체가 뼈에서 쏙 뜯겼어. 뼈마디에 매달린 힘줄이 제법 고무줄처럼 늘어나다가 끊어져 무라뜨의 입술을 찰싹 때리고는 입속으로 빨려

again? I won't say a word even if that means I'll die from eating something. What on earth are we gonna do with all this leftover food? I get that you're upset, but still—so violently—"

I lock the bedroom door and throw myself on the bed. Tear at my hair, I start to cry.

At dawn on an empty stomach and half an hour after each meal. Every two hours in between meals, and just before bed. The day flies by as I pay attention to taking my medication, seven or eight times a day. It's as though the sole purpose of my existence were to take the meds, when they don't do much to improve my condition anyway. My mother told me when I was leaving that time would take care of everything. Since the world goes round and round, any favors I get from someone and can't return in kind, I can pay it forward to someone else. And if I had a grudge from being done wrong by someone, I should consider it as canceling out a transgression I committed against someone else. Yet the more I think about what she says, the less consoling it feels to me. Maybe it was a kind of warning that you end up paying for what you do one way or another. I don't

들어갔어.

앉은 채로 점점 미끄러져 나는 엉덩이를 의자 가장자리에 간신히 걸친 채 비스듬히 누운 자세가 되었어. 그 경계만 넘으면 바닥에 엉덩방아를 찧을 판이라 의자 등받이에 뒷목을 걸고 버티고 있지. 불편하지만 고쳐 앉기마저 귀찮아. 다리를 뻗어 느슨하게 꼬고 두 손을 깍지끼어 배 위에 올려놓았어. 나 자신이 그 수북했던 갈비찜을 먹어치운 듯이 뿌듯해. 늘 찬바람 돌던 배 속에 불이라도 지펴진 것 같아. 사지가 언 빨래 녹듯 늘어져버렸어. 세상은 평화롭고 나는 노곤해.

콜레스테롤, 포화지방산, 산화효소 등등 해로운 성분과 기능에 대한 위협적인 건강 상식을 깡그리 무시하고, 무라뜨는 비계를 특히 좋아해. 고기 맛은 비계 맛이래. 그가 비계를 뽀드득뽀드득 씹는 소리를 듣고 있노라면 나는 황홀해. 오로지 혀의 명령에 따라 뭐든 듬뿍 쏟아 넣고 푹푹 끓여버리는 무라뜨의 무지막지한 요리법에 나는 반해버렸어. 음식에 대한 아무런 금기가 없는 그로서는 먹고 싶다는 단순한 욕구만으로 다른 생명을 죽이고 해할 수 있는 충분한 이유가 돼. 그 대상이 정신을 소유했건 안 했건, 마음이 있건 없건, 고통을 느끼

know of anyone who begrudges me, but my stomach problem won't grant me peace even for one day. Time heals? Although the winter's almost over, there's no sign of spring at all.

Chunks of fat-heavy meat jiggle on their own even if you pick them up ever so gently. The tablecloth has two spots from the sauce. The first, when the meat dangled down heavily from the thin bone, and the second when it sprang back up on its own. Murat quickly scoops up both spots with his fingertip and sucks them up. Then, as he catches the third drop of sauce with his outstretched tongue, he bites into the meat. There is a brief moment of tension between the meat and his teeth, but insipidly, the entire chunk of meat is soon torn away from the bone. The tendon on the bone stretches quite a bit like a rubber band before it snaps and slaps Murat on his lips as it is sucked into his mouth.

I have gradually slid in my chair to the point where I am now almost reclining, my butt barely hanging on to the edge of the seat. Any further and my butt will hit the floor, so I'm propping myself up by hooking my neck over the back of the chair. It's uncomfortable, but it's too much hassle to sit up. I

건 말건, 생명의 가능성이 얼마큼이건, 세포 수가 하나이건 무수히 많건, 죄책감 없이 먹을 수 있다니 이 얼마나 자유로운가!

무라뜨의 짧은 머리카락 새로 두피에 맺혀 있는 땀방울들이 반짝여. 귀밑으로 땀이 흘러내려 목에 죽죽 선을 남기고 있어. 암만 먹어대도 탄탄하기만 한 그의 몸을 나는 졸린 눈으로 더듬었어. 저 홀쭉한 배 속에 든 위는 들어오는 게 없어서 문제지 그만 집어넣으라고 엄살을 떠는 법은 절대로 없다고 했어. 두툼하게 까졌으면서 아래위 입술이 맞닿는 데부터는 속살처럼 생생한 분홍빛인 저 큰 입은 결코 만족할 줄을 모르지. 돼지고기를 앞뒤로 양념을 발라가며 지져서 소스를 넣어 자글자글 끓인 찜요리 한 냄비, 마늘과 양파를 듬뿍 넣고 윤이 반지르르 돌게 볶아낸 쇠고기볶음 한 접시를 다 먹어치우고도 여전히 식탐으로 번질거려.

내가 세든 집 근처에 사원이 하나 있지. 동네마다 몇 채씩 있게 마련인 작고 볼품없는 사원이야. 일부러 찾지 않으면 지나쳐버리기 십상이지. 그래도 해질녘만 되면 북을 치고 종을 울려 골목을 떠들썩하게 해. 열린 문틈으로 기웃거려보면 알록달록한 색전구에다 금박 은

stretch my legs to cross them at the ankles, put my hands over my belly and cross my fingers. I feel proud, as though I've finished off the heaping bowl of rib stew myself. A warm fire seems to be settling in my stomach instead of the chilly winds that usually whirl inside. My body feels relaxed, like just thawed frozen laundry. The world is peaceful, and I'm blissfully tired.

With a complete disregard for frightening health information on detrimental substances like cholesterol, saturated fatty acids, and oxidizing enzymes, Murat is particularly fond of fat. He says that's why he eats meat. I am enraptured listening to him chew on the fat. I have fallen for Murat's savage method of cooking, which seems to involve throwing in a whole lot of anything solely by the dictate of the tongue, then boiling the hell out of it. Since he has no taboos on food whatsoever, a simple craving for food can be reason enough to hurt and kill other living beings. Whether they have a soul or not; whether they have a heart or not; whether they can feel pain or not; however much or little chance at life they might have; whether they have one cell or an infinite number of them. To be able to eat them with absolutely no feelings of guilt—

박 장식으로 안은 꽤 현란해. 안개보다 짙은 향 연기 속에서 사람들이 앉았다 일어섰다 절을 올리고 있어. 두 손을 모아 이마에 댄 모습들이 간절해서 구경꾼인 나로서는 감히 끼어들 엄두가 나지 않아. 저토록 지성으로 빈다면, 백화점의 마네킹보다 화장이 짙은 신들일지라도 뭔가 해주지 않고는 못 배길 것 같아. 사원 바깥으로 향해진 마이크에서 나오는 찬가는 후렴구가 꼭 세 번씩 반복되지. 오 신이여, 신이여, 신이여!

문전에서 서성이다 보면 문 위의 쟁반 같은 것이 눈에 걸려. 흙으로 빚어진 접시에 커다랗게 벌어진 입과 부릅뜬 두 눈이 검고 붉게 색칠되어 있어. 그것이 '영광의 얼굴'이라고 사람들이 말했어. 먹을 게 없으니까 자신의 사지를 먹어치우고 머리통만 남은 괴물이라고. 도저히 채워질 수 없는 가공할 굶주림으로 어떤 악마건 삼켜버리기 때문에 사원을 수호한다고 했어. 동굴처럼 벌어진 그 입이.

"실제로 자기 자신을 먹는 병이 있어요. 내가 얘기했던가요? 태내에서 부모의 성병에 감염되어 자기의 팔다리를 물어뜯는 희한한 병을 갖고 태어나는 아이들이 있대요. 그러지 못하게 손발을 묶어두면 자기 입술이라

how liberating!

Through Murat's cropped hair, I see sweat glistening on his scalp. The sweat runs down behind his ears and leaves trails on his neck. My sleepy eyes grope his body, which is always hard no matter how much he eats. He has said his stomach inside that lean abdomen of his never complains about being stuffed; if anything, it doesn't get enough. That mouth, puffy and vivid pink where the lips meet, is never satisfied. It still shines with hunger despite the fact that Murat's finished off a simmering pot of pork that's been stewed with sauce, and then sautéed and brushed all over with seasonings. To top that off he's also had a plate of succulent, glossy stir fried beef and generous helpings of garlic and onion.

There is a temple near the place I'm renting. It's one of those small, humble-looking temples every village has a few of. You'd probably pass it by unless you looked for it. But every sundown, these temples fill the street with the loud sound of drums and bells. When I peep in through a crack in the door, I see it's quite dazzling inside, with colorful lights and gold and silver ornaments. People are bowing, sitting down and getting back up again, in

도 야금야금 씹어먹는다는 거예요."

대충 훑어 먹은 고기 뼈다귀를 게슴츠레한 눈으로 감상하면서 무라뜨가 말했어. 그리고 뼈다귀를 통째로 입에 넣어버렸어. 울룩불룩 뺨이 부풀어.

"그럼 어떻게 해요? 그냥 두면 그 아이들은 자기 자신을 먹어버리나요?"

"몰라요. 정 먹을 게 없으면 자기라도 먹어야지 어쩌겠어요."

그의 입에서 튀어나오는 말은 절반은 농담이고 나머지는 비아냥거림이야.

"아이들이야 죄가 없잖아요. 부모가 성병에 걸렸는데 왜 아이들이 자기를 물어뜯어야 하지요?"

"부모가 먹고 싶은 게 많아서 걸신이 들렸으니까, 낄낄."

무라뜨는 나팔을 부는 것처럼 입술을 내밀고 말갛게 씻긴 뼈다귀를 장난스럽게 뱉아냈어. 그리고 별안간 억울한 듯이 소리치는 거야.

"왜 그런 병이 생긴다고 생각해요? 성이 문란해서? 천만에! 못하게 하니까 그런 거예요. 어차피 할 수밖에 없는 걸 이것도 안 된다, 저것도 안 된다, 자꾸 금기들을

the midst of the smoke from the incense, thicker than a fog. The way they arrange their hands together at their forehead looks so earnest that a mere spectator like me wouldn't dare join in. The gods, even while wearing make-up heavier than a department store mannequin, couldn't help but be moved to do something in answer to such whole-hearted prayers. The devotional songs playing over the speakers facing outside the temple always repeat the same refrain three times: *Om namah shivaya, om namah shivaya, om namah shivaya!*

Something that looks like a big platter over the door catches your eyes when you hang out by the entrance. It's a plate made of clay, its mouth and eyes wide-open and colored black and red. People told me it is the "face of glory." They said it's a monster who's devoured his own body save for his head, because there was nothing else to eat. Thanks to its formidable, ravenous, and insatiable appetite, it protects the temple by swallowing any and all demons. It protects the temple with its mouth that's open like a cave.

"There're actually a disorder where you eat your own body. Did I tell you about it? Supposedly there are children born with this weird disorder of

만들어내니까. 알아요? 모든 성적 금기란 사회적인 억압을 정당화하기 위한 말장난에 불과해요."

결혼하기 전에는 여자하고 자면 죄가 되고, 사제 앞에서 결혼식을 올리고 난 후에는 여자하고 자야만 되는 이유는? 버스 안에서 여자 엉덩이만 만져도 파렴치범으로 몰리는데 돈이 많아 부인을 갈아치우는 건 되레 자랑인 까닭은? 대학에서 백인 남학생과 유색인 여학생 커플은 적지 않은데 그 반대의 경우는 거의 없는 이유는? 무라뜨는 내가 성 정책 담당자라도 되는 듯이 날카롭게 추궁을 해대는 거야.

"사람이 안 먹고는 못 살 듯이 그것도 안 하고는 살 수가 없잖아요. 누구나 다 하고 싶고, 또 해야만 하지요. 그런데 힘 있는 놈들이 윤리니 도덕이니 해가면서 그걸 독점하니까, 못하는 사람들은 어쩌겠어요? 하려면 비도덕적일 수밖에 없지. 그럼 도대체 누가 비윤리적인 거냐구요. 애초부터 거기에는 옳고 그르다는 절대적인 기준이란 게 있을 수가 없다는 얘기죠. 내 말은, 그러니까……"

무라뜨는 뭔가 말하려다 고깃덩이로 입을 틀어막았어. 질겅질겅 맹렬히 씹고 꿀꺽 삼킨 뒤에 말했어.

biting their own limbs because as a fetus they were infected with STDs. If you tie them up to keep them from doing it, they'll supposedly chew on their own lips."

Murat says all of this while squinting and admiring a lightly picked bone. Then he tosses the entire bone into his mouth. His cheeks bulge here and there.

"What do you do then? If you just leave them be, do those kids just eat themselves up?"

"I don't know. I guess you have to eat yourself if there's absolutely nothing else to eat."

Half of what comes out of his mouth is a joke, the other half sarcasm.

"The kids aren't at fault, though. Why do the children have to bite their own flesh when it's the parents who got the STDs in the first place?"

"Because the parents have been possessed by a demon of appetite," Murat chuckles.

Puckering his lips as if to blow on a horn, Murat playfully removes the bone from his mouth, now stripped clean. Then, all of a sudden, he shouts as if suddenly upset about something unfair.

"Why do you think they get those diseases? Cause they're sexually promiscuous? Not at all! It's

"난 더 먹어야겠어요."

며칠은 굶은 사람처럼 그는 얼굴빛마저 창백해졌어. 나도 어지러워. 무라뜨의 성토를 뒤집어쓴 얼굴이 화끈거리고 위도 더부룩해. 음식 구경이야 실컷 했지만 정작 먹은 건 없는데도 과식한 것처럼 속이 부대껴. 쌕쌕 숨을 몰아쉬며 나는 식탁 위의 후춧병과 그을음 탄 찬장문과, 똑똑 물이 떨어지고 있는 개수대의 수도꼭지를 둘러보았어. 결국 내 눈은 무라뜨의 다리로 돌아왔어. 내 발에 닿지 않으려고 그의 다리는 탁자 옆으로 비어져 나와 있어. 장작개비처럼 깡마른 다리를 뒤덮은 돌돌 말린 털들이 무척 부드러워 보여. 이 공기 나쁜 도시에서 맨발로 조깅할 일도 없을 텐데 왜 발가락 마디마다 못이 박였을까. 모르겠어, 그가 고향에서는 사슴처럼 들판을 뛰어다녔는지. 발등과 발바닥이 만나는 옆구리에 선이 한 줄 그어져 있어. 그 위로 발등은 검고 그 밑으로 발바닥은 희어. 그 대비가 하도 뚜렷해서 나는 그 부위에 내 손을 대봐야 할 것만 같은 기분이 들어.

발을 화들짝 끌어당기면서 무라뜨는 일어났어. 빈 접시들을 쓸어다 개수대에 담가놓고 김이 오르는 솥에서 뭔가를 그릇에 퍼냈어. 식탁에 날라 온 걸 보니 생선살

because they're forbidden to have any sex. You're bound to do it anyway, yet they keep handing you all these bans, saying you can't do this, you can't do that, you know? All sexual taboos are nothing more than verbal tricks to justify societal oppression."

Why is it a sin to have premarital sex with a woman but you have to sleep with a woman once you're married before clergy? How come you're branded a pervert if you so much as touch a woman's bottom on a bus, yet it's something to boast about if you can replace your wife with someone else because you're rich enough to afford it? Why are there more than a few couples involving white male students and female students of color in college, but hardly any opposite pairings? Murat grills me as if I were some bureaucrat in charge of sexual policy.

"Just like you can't live without eating, you can't live without doing it, right? Everyone wants to do it, and should. But those powerful SOBs monopolize it under the pretext of ethics and morality. What are the rest of us to do? If you're gonna do it, you'll have to be immoral. Then let me ask you, which is the unethical side? What I'm saying is there can't be any absolute standards of right and wrong

을 부서뜨려 넣고 야채와 함께 끓인 쌀죽이야. 냄새가 기가 막혀. 그러나 아니나 다를까 그는 죽을 한 그릇 더 퍼서 내 앞에 놓았어. 아아, 또 시작이야. 왜 그는 자기 잔치에 나까지 끌어들이려는지 모르겠어. 내 앞에서 과시하듯이 고깃덩어리를 뜯는 것도 나를 자극해보려는 속셈이요, 본래 목적은 그다음에 등장하는 특별 요리를 내게 먹이는 거야.

그가 주변에 묻기도 하고 나름대로 연구도 해가면서 내 위장병에 좋은 음식을 만드느라 애를 쓰고 있다는 걸 나도 알아. 닭을 뼈째 고아 냉장고에 넣었다가 기름을 걷어낸 걸쭉한 곰국, 쇠고기와 양배추 스튜, 돼지갈비와 사과를 흐무러지도록 푹 끓인 희한한 탕, 쌀과 함께 다진 쇠고기를 볶아 우유와 설탕, 이름 모를 약초를 넣어 달달하게 끓인 죽, 나로서는 국적도 모르겠는 환자용 보양식들을 그는 차례로 선보였어. 그러나 나는 먹을 수가 없는걸. 고기 냄새를 맡으면 회가 동하다가도 막상 입에 넣으려면 메스껍다는 말을 도대체 몇 번이나 해야 되는지 모르겠어. 나한테 미리 물어봤으면 하지 말라고나 했지. 하긴 그래봤자 그는 절대로 내 말을 귀담아듣지 않을 테지만.

when it comes to that in the first place. So—"

Murat is about to say something, but he stuffs his mouth with a chunk of meat instead. He chews vigorously and swallows loudly. Then he says:

"I'm going to eat some more."

His face turns pale as if he'd starved for days. I'm dizzy, too. My face feels hot after getting smeared by Murat's protests, and even my stomach is uncomfortable. I haven't eaten anything, though I've seen food to my heart's content. But my stomach feels upset as if I'd overeaten. Breathing with difficulty, I look around at the pepper mill on the table, the scorched cupboard doors, and the faucet that's leaking drop after drop of water. Eventually, my eyes come back to Murat's legs. They're sticking out the sides of the table so they won't touch my feet. The curly hair that covers his boney legs looks very soft. There can't be many occasions to jog barefoot in this polluted city, so I wonder how all the knuckles of his toes are calloused. I don't know, maybe he ran around the field like a deer back in his hometown. There's a line on the side of his feet where the bottom meets the top. It is black above it, and pale below. The contrast is so stark that I feel compelled to touch that area with my

역시 위경련이 일기 시작했어. 나는 배를 감싸 쥐고 위의 움직임에 신경을 곤두세웠어. 힐뜩 내 눈치를 보더니 무라뜨의 표정이 굳었어. 얼른 죽 그릇에 코를 박아버리는 거야.

"왜요? 뭐 잘못된 거 있어요?"

나는 부루퉁하게 물었어. 내가 한마디 하기도 전에 왜 제가 먼저 토라지느냐 말이야.

"……"

물론 무라뜨는 고개를 젓지. 그러나 얼굴이 검붉게 달아올랐는걸.

"내가 당신 요리를 안 먹어서 기분 나쁜 거예요? 걱정해주는 건 정말 고마운데요, 비린내 나는 건 못 먹겠는 걸 어떻게 해요."

"내가 만든 건 모조리 당신한테 역겹죠."

"미안해요. 하지만 좀 이해해줄 수 없어요? 위가 안 받는 걸 어쩌란 말예요. 나중에 무슨 고생을 하든 당신이 일단 만들어놓은 건 내가 다 먹어야 한다 이거예요? 먹고 죽을지언정……"

"……"

무라뜨가 이를 악물었어. 소리를 내지는 않았지만 입

hand.

Murat gets up, pulling in his feet with a jolt. He collects the empty plates, puts them in the sink, and dishes out something steaming from the pot. When he puts it on the table, I can see that it's rice porridge made with vegetables and crumbled fish filet. It smells divine. But then he has to dish out another bowl and put it in front of me. Ugh. Here we go again. Why does he want to drag me into his feast, I wonder? All the gloating bites into chunks of meat right in front of me were to get a rise out of me; his real objective is to feed me the special dish that comes next.

I do know that he tries to cook food that's good for my stomach problem by asking around and doing his own research. He has so far presented me with a string of healing dishes of uncertain origin, such as a thick chicken broth made by broiling a whole boned chicken to a pulp and skimming off the fat after cooling it in the fridge, a beef and vegetable stew, a unique overcooked stew of pork ribs and apples, and a sweet porridge made by first frying white rice with minced beef and then boiling them together with milk, sugar, and herbs whose names I don't even know. But I simply can't eat

술 새로 흰 이빨이 반짝여. 으르렁거리는 짐승이야. 나는 입을 다물었어. 아무리 분통이 터져도 그는 나처럼 부엌에서 뛰쳐나가지는 않을 거야. 육식이 금지된 기숙사에서 배를 곯는 그에게는 내 부엌이 꼭 필요하기 때문이지. 어떤 슬픔이나 분노도 능가하는, 당장 먹어야겠다는 그의 절실한 요구 앞에서 나는 눈을 내리깔았어. 그의 다리가 도로 탁자 옆으로 나와 있어.

"왜요? 왜 그렇게 고기는 안 된다는 거죠? 드디어 채식주의자가 되기로 작정했나요?"

이지러진 얼굴에 능글맞은 웃음을 덧씌우며 그가 물었어. 매우 느리고 한 음절마다 발음이 분명한 그 말투에는 그가 아까 '독점하려는 놈들'이라고 말했을 때처럼 독특한 느낌이 있어. 독점하려는 채식주의자. 다모를 암시, 아니 노골적으로 들먹이고 있는 거지.

우리는 할 말을 다 해버린 기분으로 서로를 바라보았어. 언제나 우리 얘기는 그 어떤 채식주의자, 다모에서 끝나지. 뺨이 홀쭉하게 패고 입꼬리가 늘어진 무라뜨는 오늘따라 중년처럼 나이 들어 보여. 그 어느 때보다 허기진 것 같아.

them. While I do get an appetite upon smelling meat, when it comes to actually putting it in my mouth, I keep saying over and over how nauseating it is. I could at least tell him not to bother if he'd ask me beforehand. I suppose, though, that he wouldn't listen to me anyway.

As expected, I start getting stomach cramps. Cradling my belly with my hands, I become ultra-sensitive to the activities in my stomach. Murat's face is frozen after he catches me with a quick look. He dunks his nose into the porridge bowl right away.

"What is it? Something wrong?"

I ask sullenly. Why does he get sulky before I even say a word? Of course, he shakes his head. But his face is black and red.

"Are you mad that I didn't eat the food you've cooked? I appreciate your concern for me, but I just can't eat anything that has that raw meat smell."

"Everything I make grosses you out."

"I'm sorry, but can't you be a little understanding? Can I help it if my stomach won't take it? Or are you saying I have to eat whatever you've made for me, no matter how much pain I might be in later? Eat and die even..."

Murat clenches his jaw. He makes no sound, but

오늘도 엄청나게 불행한 일이 다모에게 생겼어. 현관에 들어서는 그의 얼굴에 역력히 씌어 있지. 왜 사람들은 제가 먼저 제의했던 약속조차 잊어버리고, 그래놓고는 더욱 괘씸하게 사과가 아니라 되지도 않는 변명을 하며, 빌려갔던 녹음기를 고장내놓고 모르는 척 돌려주고, 어린 티를 갓 벗은 점원은 잔돈푼을 슬그머니 떼어먹는 것부터 배우는가? 왜 이 나라 정부는 순전히 명분뿐인 국수주의 경제정책을 고집하여 환율을 비정상적으로 묶어놓는가? 오늘 암시장의 달러 환율은 말이 안 된다. 이 도시에서 딱 한 군데 시장에서만 파는 두부는 왜 날이 갈수록 작아지는가? 왜? 왜? 왜?

"어?"

오전 동안에만도 무수하게 겪은 불쾌한 일들에 분통을 터뜨리며 세면대의 수도꼭지를 비틀던 다모가 멈칫했어. 각오를 하고 있었음에도 불구하고 나는 눈앞이 캄캄해졌어. 이제 이골이 날 때도 됐건만 나는 그의 화난 얼굴만 보면 매번 심장이 졸아들어.

"……물이 안 나와요. 하필 음식을 하느라고 받아놓은 물을 다 쓰고 나니까."

"더 이상 얘기하기도 지쳤어요, 난. 일에는 순서가 있

I can see his white teeth flash between his lips. He's a roaring beast. I shut my mouth. No matter how frustrated he gets, he won't bolt out of the kitchen like me. He positively needs my kitchen because he starves at the dorm where eating meat is prohibited. I glance down, yielding to his desperate demand to eat immediately, which supersedes any rage or sorrow. His legs are sticking out the sides of the table again.

"Why? Why are you so averse to meat? Have you finally decided to become a vegetarian?"

A sly smile comes over his contorted face. His tone, very slow, with every syllable enunciated, has a distinctive feel similar to when he said "those monopolizing SOBs." The monopolizing vegetarian. He's hinting at—no, quite explicitly referring to—Damo.

We look at each other, feeling that we've said everything we need to say. Our conversation always ends up on that certain vegetarian. Damo. With his gaunt cheeks and his mouth turned down at the ends, Murat looks particularly old today, like a middle-aged man. He looks more famished than ever.

A tragic thing happened to Damo again today. His face shows it clearly as he steps into my apartment.

는 법이에요. 밥이야 한두 끼 안 먹을 수도 있고 나중에 먹을 수도 있는 걸. 물부터 받아놔야지. 전기건 수도건 하루에도 몇 번씩 들어왔다 말았다 하는 줄 뻔히 알면서. 당장 손 씻을 물도 없단 말예요?"

"욕조에 좀 남았을 거예요."

"좀? 우선 화장실은 어쩔 거예요? 나야 기숙사로 돌아가면 그만이지만."

"안 돼요!"

"그럼 어쩌자는 말이에요? 오늘은 분명히 뭔가 잘못돼도…… 그렇지 않고서야 하루 종일……"

분명히 음모가 있어, 그렇지 않고서야 어떻게 내게는 나쁜 일만 생길 수가 있겠어? 세상은 나만 미워해. 다모는 내가 그에게 적대적인 세상 그 자체라도 된다는 듯이 쏘아보았어.

"미안해요!"

나는 가슴이 저렸어. 그에게는 정말 되는 일이 하나도 없으니 옆에서 보는 내가 다 민망해. 매사에 그의 일이 꼬일 때마다 나는 그걸 내가 보상이라도 해줘야 할 것처럼 죄스러워지는 거야.

어떤 음식이건 몸에 안 좋다는 얘기를 한 번만 들으

Why do people forget promises that they suggested first? And then, to make things worse, in place of apologies they give excuses that make no sense. Why do they borrow recorders, break them, and return them like they're unaware of it? Why does a cashier barely out of puberty first learn to "forget" to give you the right change? Why does the government of this nation insist on an economic policy that's only for show, locking in the abnormal exchange rate? Today's black market exchange rate for the dollar is ridiculous. Why does the tofu at the only place in the city that sells it keep getting smaller by the day? Why? Why? Why?

"Huh?"

Damo, venting about the numerous unpleasant events he encountered in the morning alone, pauses while turning the faucet of the bathroom sink. Although I braced myself for it, I'm rattled. It's time I got used to it, but my heart recoils whenever I see his face angry.

"...There's no water. Happened just after I used up all the water I'd drawn for cooking."

"I'm tired of talking to you about it. There's an order to doing things, you know. You can skip a meal or two, or have it later. You should collect

면 평생 다시 입에 대는 법이 없고, 건강 유지를 가장 큰 업으로 삼는 그가 왜 노상 갖가지 질병에 시달려야 할까. 아침에 일어나면 방부터 싹싹 쓸고 남방셔츠 칼라를 빳빳하게 다리며, 다리미가 식기 전에 손수건도 반듯하게 누른다는 그가 왜 왠지 추레하게 보여야만 하는가 말이야. 샴푸와 로션은 반이 채 비기도 전에 거꾸로 세워놓고, 여벌로 비누나 치약을 서랍 가득 채워놓았으며, 비상시를 대비해서 끓는 물만 부으면 되는 즉석식품도 몇 봉지쯤 기숙사 침대 밑에 넣어둔 그, 장래에 대한 계획과 준비에 최선을 다하는 다모가 왜 늘 얄궂은 불운에 조롱당해야 할까.

얼마 전 고국에서 사촌 매제의 동업자가 사기를 당하는 바람에 그도 적지 않은 피해를 입었다고 했어. 날마다 입가에 침이 허옇게 말라붙도록 조바심을 치건만 그가 미연에 방지할 수 있는 불행은 하나도 없고, 인간을 향한 그의 선의는 간단히 무시당하지. 안간힘을 쓸수록 더 나쁜 결과만 얻게 되는 이 부당한 현실은 누구의 책임인가?

식탁에 앉아서도 다모는 기분 나빴던 일들만 되새김하고 있어. 이를 악물었는지 귀 옆으로 근육이 불거지

water first. You know only too well that electricity and water can go in and out several times a day. Do you mean there's not even any water for washing hands?"

"There should be a little bit left in the tub."

"A little bit? To begin with, how will you go to the bathroom? I mean, I could just go back to the dorm."

"No!"

"Then what do you want to do? Something must be up today... otherwise, how can things, all day long—"

This must be a conspiracy. Otherwise, how can only bad things happen to me? The world hates me only. Damo glares at me as if I were that antagonistic world itself.

"I'm sorry!"

I have pangs of heart. He really has bad luck, making me sorry when I'm only a bystander. Whenever everything goes wrong for him, I feel guilty, as if I need to compensate for it.

Once he hears that a certain food is bad for you, he'll avoid it for the rest of his life. His most time-consuming activity is maintenance of his health. So why is he always suffering from all kinds of diseas-

고 관자놀이에서 푸른 정맥이 볼록거려. 목에는 아직도 손수건이 친친 감겨 있어. 하루가 다르게 날씨가 풀려 후텁지근한 판에 목을 동여맨 그 모습을 보는 내가 너무 갑갑해.

"이럴 때일수록 억지로라도…… 조금만 더 먹어요, 네?"

그의 주의를 음식으로 돌려보려고 나는 요리접시를 옮겨놓기도 하고 내 몫의 흰죽을 떠먹기도 했어.

"……"

그래봤자 다모는 꿈쩍도 하지 않아. 식탁 위의 음식들은 내가 아무리 애를 써봤자 그에게 조금도 위로가 되지 않는다는 걸 증명하기 위해 전시돼 있는 것만 같아. 송곳이라도 쑤셔박힌 듯이 내 가슴이 미어져. 그를 위해 무슨 짓이라도 하지 않으면 숨이 막혀버릴 것만 같아. 그가 음식을 거부하면 할수록 나는 당장 그에게 뭐라도 먹이지 않으면 큰일 날 것처럼 더욱더 애가 타.

"제발 맛이라도 좀 봐요. 토마토가 감기에 좋대요. 특히 남자한테 더 좋다던데요."

"누가 그래요?"

"……"

es? He sweeps his room the first thing in the morning, he says, irons the collars of his shirts straight, as well as his handkerchiefs before the iron cools down. So why must he still look shabby somehow? He puts the shampoo and lotion bottles upside down even before they're half empty, stocks his drawers with back-up soap and toothpaste, and, just in case of an emergency, even keeps under his bed at his dorm several containers of instant food that only need boiling water. Why must Damo, who does his best to plan and prepare for his future, be so mocked by perverse misfortune?

He told me that the business partner of his cousin by marriage got swindled back home a while ago, causing him substantial damage as well. He's a worrywart to the point of having dried-up saliva around his mouth every day, yet there is not one instance of bad luck that he can prevent, his goodwill toward humanity ignored just like that. Who is responsible for this unjust situation, where the more you exert yourself, the worse your results get?

Seated at the table, Damo is ruminating on only the bad things. He must be clenching his teeth, for I can see muscles protruding around the sides of

후드득 나는 눈물을 떨구고야 말았어. 토마토가 남자한테 좋다는 말은 무라뜨한테 들었거든. 무슨 얘기를 하건 우리의 대화는 결국 무라뜨를 들먹이게 돼. 무라뜨는 1, 2주일에 한 번씩 내 부엌을 잠깐 빌릴 뿐이건만, 다모와 내가 식탁에 앉을 때마다 그도 함께 있는 거나 마찬가지야. 우리는 무라뜨에 대해서만 생각하고 그에 관한 얘기만 하거든. 하지만 결코 그의 이름이 직접 나오진 않지. 무라뜨라는 석 자를 빈칸으로 남겨놓고 얘기가 그 주위를 돌고 또 돌아.

"이것만은 알아줘요. 나는 당신을 행복하게 해주고 싶을 뿐이에요."

나는 울먹이며 자리에서 일어났어. 다모에게 다가가 그의 목을 조르고 있는 손수건을 마침내 풀어냈지.

"뭐 그럴 필요야 없어요. 당신한테 그런 것까지 바라지도 않아요. 다만 나를 더욱 비참하게 만들지만……"

그의 냉랭한 대답에 절로 무릎이 꺾였어. 나는 스르르 바닥으로 무너져 내렸어. 더 이상의 독설을 듣지 않으려고 나는 그의 바지 앞섶을 헤치고 팬티를 잡아 내렸어. 수줍은 그의 성기를 끌어내어 입에 넣어버렸지. 그는 흠칫 몸이 굳더니 이내 그 어느 때보다도 심하게 인

his ears, the blue veins popping near his temples. A scarf is still wrapped round and round his neck. With the weather getting warmer by the day—it's kind of sultry now—I'm stifled just looking at his tightly bound neck.

"At times like this, especially—make yourself eat just a bit more, will you please?"

I try to switch his attention to food by moving the plates around; I even eat some of my white rice porridge.

Still, Damo does not move a muscle. The plates on the table seem to be on display as proof that no matter how hard I try, I can never comfort him. My heart is distress, as though it were stuffed and wadded with cotton. I feel I may suffocate if I don't do something for him. The more he refuses food, the more I burn with impatience, feeling there'll be a big catastrophe if I don't feed him something soon.

"Please have just a taste. Tomatoes are supposed to be good for colds. Especially for men."

"Says who?"

Instead of answering, I end up crying a few tears. It was Murat who told me tomatoes are good for men. Whatever we talk about, we end up bringing him up. Though he merely borrows my kitchen

상을 썼어. 얼굴이 자주색으로 물들고 입술이 부들부들 떨렸지.

"당신은 나를 죽이려는군요. 죽이려고 해요…… 나도 알아요, 당신이 날 얼마나 미워하는지……"

거칠어진 숨결로 간신히, 그러나 쉴 새 없이 그는 중얼거렸어. 다모가 더욱 불행해지지 않으려면 무라뜨가 내 부엌에서 고기 요리를 해먹지 말아야 한다는, 이 난해한 공식을 나는 도저히 이해할 수가 없어. 다모가 상처 입지 않기 위해서는 무라뜨가 굶주려야 한다니. 왜 항상 문제는 가장 나쁜 방식으로, 꼭 누군가를 패배자로 만들며 풀려야 하는지. 나는 얼굴을 다모의 허벅지 새에 묻은 채로 두 손을 그의 남방셔츠 안으로 밀어넣었어. 혁대에 졸린 러닝셔츠를 빼내고 그의 맨살을 더듬었어.

"아, 아, 죽겠어요, 정말, 죽어버릴 것 같아요……"

다모는 의자에서 점점 미끄러져 내렸어. 의자 끄트머리에 엉덩이가 간신히 걸려 있어.

"차라리 나를 죽여요…… 그게 낫겠어요, 나를 더 이상…… 고문하지 말아요……"

나는 열렬히 고민했어. 다모한테는 활짝 열린 내 부엌

briefly every week or two, Murat is virtually present whenever Damo and I sit down at the table. We only think about Murat, only talk about Murat. Yet we never mention him directly by name. We just run circles around the five empty spaces for the letters in his name.

"Please know this—I just wish to make you happy."

Sniffling, I get up from my seat. I stand next to Damo and finally take off the handkerchief choking his neck.

"No, there's no need. I don't even want that from you. I just ask that you don't make me even more pathetic—"

His cold reply brings me to my knees almost automatically. I fall down, gliding to the floor. In order not to hear any more of his venomous words, I open the fly of his pants and pull down his underwear. I pull out his shy penis and put it in my mouth. His body freezes up for a moment, then his face grimaces more strongly than ever. His face is purple, his lips shaking uncontrollably.

"You're trying to kill me. You want to kill me—I know how much you hate me—"

With quickened breath, he barely, yet unceasingly

이 무라뜨한테는 닫혀야 하는 이유는? 이유는? 이유는? 집 근처 사원에서 울려나오는 찬가의 삼박자가 머릿속에 박혀버렸어. 무라뜨가 헌신적일수록 내가 그에게 잔인해지고, 다모가 가혹할수록 그에게는 더욱 비굴해지는 까닭은? 까닭은? 까닭은?

"그, 그…… 그만, 정말 주…… 죽겠다구요!"

다모는 눈을 질끈 감고 왼쪽 오른쪽으로 고개를 마구 내저었어. 밑에서 올려다보는 내게는 그의 턱뼈가 각이 지고 입술이 부풀어 보여. 자기에게 이런 끔찍한 일이 닥쳤다는 걸 믿을 수 없다는 듯한, 그러면서도 싫지는 않은 듯한 표정이야. 그가 화나 있지 않은 유일한 순간이야.

나는 저런 표정을 알아. 무라뜨가 사진을 보여주었거든. 사원의 장식물 얘기가 나오자 그는 또 열심히 연구를 했던가봐. 고대 종교 제의에 쓰였던 '영광의 얼굴'들의 사진첩을 빌려다 주었어. 거기에 괴물이 두 앞발로 사람을 움켜쥐고 막 삼키려는 모습의 조각상이 실려 있어. 괴물한테 먹히는 사람이 바로 저런 표정을 짓고 있었어. 자기 머리가 시방 괴물의 이빨에 와작 씹힐 찰나인데도 그 사람은 몽롱해 보였어. 고통과 환희를 동시

mutters this. I cannot for the life of me understand this complex equation where in order to save Damo from further misfortune Murat cannot cook meat in my kitchen. Murat has to starve for Damo not to get hurt. Why does every problem get solved in the worst possible way, always turning somebody into a loser? Keeping my face buried between his thighs, I push my hands up under Damo's shirt. I untuck the undershirt from his belt, and caress his bare skin.

"Oh. Oh. I'm dying, really. I'm gonna die—"

Damo keeps sliding from his chair. His butt is barely hanging onto the edge of the seat.

"Why don't you just kill me instead... that would be better. Please don't... torture me any more—"

I'm in serious anguish. My kitchen, wide open to Damo, has to be closed off to Murat: why does it? Why does it? Why does it? I've got in my head the three-beat refrain of the devotional song that plays over at the temple near my place. The more devoted Murat is, the crueler I am towards him, while the more severe Damo is, the more pathetic I am with him: Why is it? Why is it? Why is it?

"St-stop! I'm really d-dying!"

His eyes squeezed shut, Damo keeps shaking his

에 느끼는 듯한, 그 절정에서 오히려 무감각해져버린 것 같은 얼굴이었어. 그 사진을 보았을 때 나는 지금처럼 넋을 놓아버린 다모를 떠올렸어. 아니면 그걸 본 이후에 내가 다모의 얼굴에서 그 표정을 찾기 시작했는지도 모르지만. 분노와 억울함을 놓아버린, 기쁨으로 자기를 내주고 있는 저 얼굴은 아름다워.

사진의 설명문에는 그 인물들이 희생제의의 열광적인 참여자로서 자원해서 제물이 된 사람들이라고 나와 있었어. 나도 한번 그래보고 싶어. 언젠가 한번쯤은 희생제의의 제물이 되어 열광적으로 죽어보고 싶어. 살아 있는 한 멈출 수 없는 이 노역, 자기를 방어함으로써 다른 누군가를 해치는 이 안간힘을 잠시 멈추고 싶어. 어리둥절하면서도 몽롱한 상태에서 머리통이 으스러뜨려지고 싶어. 순순히 먹혀보고 싶어. 나는 포식자(捕食者)보다는 피식자(被食者)가, 음식이 되고 싶어.

"그, 그만!"

갑자기 다모가 나를 밀쳐냈어. 그의 러닝셔츠 안에 들어가 있던 내 손이 빠져나오고 내 입에서 그의 성기가 튀어나왔지.

"그러지 말라고 내가 벌써 몇 번이나 얘기했는데, 도

head wildly left and right. From my vantage looking up, his jawbone appears angular and his lips puffy. His face seems to say he can't believe such a terrible thing has befallen him but he's not really appalled. This is also the only moment when he isn't upset.

I'm familiar with that kind of facial expression. Murat showed me a photo once. After we talked about temple ornaments, he must have studied them hard. He checked out a photo book for me once, a collection of the "faces of glory" used in ancient religious rites. The book had this carving[1)] of a monster about to eat people held in its front paws. Those people had that very same expression on their faces. They appeared dazed despite the fact that their heads were, at that instant, about to be crushed in by the monster's teeth. They seemed to be feeling pain and ecstasy at the same time. As though they had gone numb at their peak. When I saw that photo, I thought of Damo looking out of it as he is now. Or, maybe it was that I started to look for that expression in Damo after seeing that photo. It's a beautiful face, free from rage and chagrin, giving itself up to joy.

According to the photo's caption, the people, passionate participants in the sacrificial rites, had

대체 왜 그러는 거예요? 그게 재미있어요?"

그가 항의했어. 내가 또 같은 실수를 저질렀던 거야. 그는 내 손가락이 자기 배꼽에 들어가는 걸 끔찍하게 싫어해. 먼젓번에도, 그 전번에도 그의 러닝셔츠 밑으로 내 손이 들어가 그 부위에 도달했을 때, 그는 앉아 있고 나는 무릎을 꿇은 이런 상태에서 그는 화를 냈어. 그래서 나는 다음에 어떤 장면이 이어져야 하는지 알았지. 그가 분노를 잊게 만들려면 웬만한 자극으로는 안 돼. 예전의 경우처럼 나는 일어나서 옷을 홀딱 벗었어.

"당신 확실히 살이 붙었어요. 요즘 체중 재봤어요?"

다모가 내 몸을 훑어보며 말했어. 위장병으로 고생하는 내게 뚱뚱해졌다는 사람은 오직 이 사람 한 명뿐이야. 더구나 알몸으로 남자 앞에 서 있는 처지에서 상대방의 시큰둥한 반응이 어찌나 모멸스러운지, 나야말로 죽고 싶어.

"다른 덴 잘 모르겠는데요, 여기, 이 근처에 살이 몰리는 것 같아요."

다모는 내 배꼽을 겨냥해서 손가락으로 공중에다 동그라미를 여러 번이나 겹쳐 그렸어. 그러고는 자연스럽게 손을 뻗어 엄지와 검지로 내 아랫배를 집어보는 거

volunteered to be the offerings. I'd like to try that sometime. I'd like to, at some point, die a fervent death as an offering at a sacrificial rite. I'd like to pause, if only briefly, from this labor that you cannot cease as long as you're alive, this exertion to defend yourself at the expense of harming others. I'd like to have my head crushed in while in a confused daze. I'd like to be eaten agreeably without resistance. I'd rather be the eaten than the eater. I'd like to become food.

"S-stop!"

Suddenly, Damo pushes me away. My hands retreat from up under his undershirt, and his penis pops out of my mouth.

"How many times have I told you not to do that? Why on earth did you do that? Is it fun for you?"

He protests. I've committed the same mistake. He abhors having my finger in his bellybutton. The other day, when my hand beneath his undershirt reached that area, he scolded me while he was seated and I was kneeling down. So now I know what needs to follow this scene. It takes more than your average stimulus to make him forget his rage. Like before, I stand up and undress completely.

"You did get fat, for sure. Have you weighed

야. 그게 얼마나 두꺼운지, 얼마만큼의 지방층이 쌓였는지를 재보려는 거지. 정확하게 측정해내려는 제법 신중한 자세야. 부드득, 내 입에서 이 갈리는 소리가 새나왔어.

그 괴물의 손아귀에 잡혀 있는 사람들은 홀가분해 보였어. 제물이 됨으로써 그들은 몸만이 아니라 다른 것도 괴물한테 떠넘길 수 있다고 생각하는 것 같았어. 마음속의 근심, 살아 있음으로써 저질렀던 피비린내 나는 죄악들까지도. 괴물은 모든 걸 삼켜줄 만큼 입이 충분히 컸어. 그래서 그 괴물과 사람은 먹고 먹힌다기보다, 어떻게 보면 어머니가 품에 아기를 부둥켜안고 있는 것처럼 보이기도 했어.

해질녘 우유통에 우유를 받아 오다가, 혹은 감자 몇 톨 사들고 오다가 그 작은 사원 앞에만 오면 나는 멈춰. 발이 붙잡힌 듯 앞으로 나가지를 않아. 입을 쩍 벌린 '영광의 얼굴'에 가로막혀 사원 안에 들어가지도 못하면서 그저 문 앞에 서 있어. 사원에서는 높낮이 다른 목소리들이 목청껏 찬가를 합창하지. 북, 종, 심벌즈 치고 탬버린까지 흔들어대며 푸닥거리가 한창이야. 신도들은 신

yourself lately?"

Says Damo, giving my body a thorough look-over. This man is the only person who tells me that I've gotten fat when I suffer from stomach problems. What's more, the nonchalant reaction from the person you're standing naked in front of is so humiliating. I'm the one who want to die.

"It's not so obvious in other spots, but here, I think around here is where you tend to hold fat."

He aims his finger at my bellybutton and keep making circles in the air. Then, extending his hand naturally, he squeezes my lower belly with his thumb and index finger. He's trying to measure how thick it is, how much fat has accumulated there. He is exhibiting quite a meticulous attitude, intent on obtaining an accurate measurement. I hear my teeth grinding.

Those people in the grip of that monster all looked relieved. By becoming the offering of the monster, they seemed to think that they could pass not only bodies but also other things on the monster. Like worries in their heart. And the blood-soaked sins they'd committed by virtue of being alive, even. The monster's mouth was big enough to

상(神像) 앞에서 서로 질세라 절들을 해대고, 사원 밖에는 차례를 기다리는 사람들이 길게 줄을 서. 저녁밥 먹기 전에 반드시 해야 할 일이라는 듯이 줄 서 있는 사람들의 얼굴에 초조감마저 어리지.

두 손을 모아 이마에 대고 사람들은 하루 동안 지은 죄를 내려놓고 가버려. 아무리 중한 죄도 성스러운 강에 가서 목욕하면 씻겨진다고 했어. 숱하게 많은 사원들에서 언제라도 속죄를 할 수 있기 때문에 사람들은 다시 죄를 지을 수가 있지. 죄를 짓지 않을 수가 없는 일상생활을 계속할 수가 있는 거야. 나는 그들을 부럽게 훔쳐봐. 고향을 떠나면서 끌고 온 마음의 짐을, 그들처럼 나도 경건하게 부려놓고 싶어. 그리고 뚜벅뚜벅 걸어 나와 저녁 먹으러 가고 싶어.

나도 그들처럼 후광이 총천연색으로 번쩍이는 신들 앞에서 앉았다 일어섰다 절하고 싶어. 어떤 신에게건, 어떤 종파의 신전에서건 나는 납작하게 엎드려 빌고 싶어. 내가 누구한테도 안 먹히고 여태껏 살아 있는 걸 용서해달라고. 나도 둥둥둥 북을 치고 땡땡땡 종을 울리며 세 번씩 반복하고 싶어. 살아 있어서 미안하다고, 미안하다고, 미안하다고.

swallow all of this. So the monster and the people looked less like the eater and the eaten, and more like a mother clasping her babies to her bosom.

On my way back from filling my jar with milk or buying a few potatoes at dusk, I always pause when I get to that temple. As if being caught, my feet just won't move forward. Barred by the "face of glory" with its mouth wide open, I can't even go inside, so I simply stand in front of the door. At the temple, all kinds of voices, from high to low, belt out devotional songs together. Drums, bells, cymbals, and tambourines join in for the animated purging ritual. While the followers compete with one another at bowing before the statues, people form long lines outside the temple for their turn to bow. There is even a hint of anxiousness on the faces of those in line, as if to say this is something that must be completed before dinner.

With their hands held together at their forehead, people let go of the sins of the day before departing. They said even the gravest sins will be washed away if you bathe in the river with holy water. It's okay to commit new sins because you can always repent at any of the ubiquitous temples. This is how they're able to keep on living their daily lives

도시가 온통 황토색이야. 하늘이 뿌옇고 나무들은 진흙을 한 꺼풀 뒤집어쓴 듯하고, 차창은 코팅이라도 된 것 같아. 사막에서 모래를 싣고 열풍이 불어닥쳤어. 지나가는 사람들은 머리카락이 부스스하고 차들이 모두 같은 색이야. 귓속에서, 입 안에서 모래가 자글거려. 아침에 다렸을 다모의 셔츠칼라도 싯누래. 오늘따라 그는 몰골이 말이 아니야. 강도처럼 손수건으로 얼굴을 가리고도 안경 속의 두 눈까지 찌푸리고 있지. 평소에는 콘택트렌즈를 끼지만 요즘처럼 바람이 많을 때는 눈을 보호하기 위해 안경을 써. 모래바람은 호흡기 질환뿐만 아니라 안질, 피부병, 알러지까지 유발한다고 그는 주장하지.

애걸이 아니라 옷자락을 잡아당기면서 협박을 하는 거지들 때문에, 도로 맞은편에 있다가 굳이 길을 건너와서까지 신분증 검사를 한 순경 때문에, 또는 다른 많은 이유들로 인해 그는 화가 나 있어. 간장 한 통 사러 가는 길에 우여곡절이 너무 많아. 그의 옆에 있으면 나는 폐를 옥죄어 들어오는 압력 같은 걸 느껴. 잠수부들이 심해에서 느낀다는 수압이 이런 느낌일 것 같아. 확확 달아오르는 그의 분노에 밀려 자꾸 몸을 움츠리게

where they cannot keep from sinning. I peek at them with envy. Like them, I also want to discharge sacredly the weight in my heart, which I dragged with me when I left home. Then march out and head for dinner.

Like them, I want to sit down and stand up over and over while bowing before the gods, their halos glowing in every possible color. I want to ask any god for forgiveness, lying flat on my stomach in a temple of whatever kind of religion. I want to be forgiven for staying alive all this time without being eaten by anyone. I, too, want to beat the drum and ring the bell while repeating the phrase three times: I'm sorry, I'm sorry, I'm sorry for being alive.

The entire city is the color of ochre. The sky is dusty, trees look like they're wearing a film of wet clay, and the windows appear coated. Heated winds have arrived carrying sand from the desert. People pass by with unkempt, straw-like hair, and the cars are all of one color. Sand crackles in my mouth, in my ears. The collar of Damo's shirt, which he most certainly ironed straight this morning, is yellow. He looks particularly pitiful today. Even with covering his face with a scarf like a bandit, he squints behind his glasses. While he usually

돼. 마늘도, 양파도, 고춧가루도 안 먹는데 그는 왜 이렇게 성미가 불같은지 나는 진정 모르겠어. 출발할 땐 택시 뒷자리에 나란히 앉아 있었건만 곧 어린애처럼 작고 마른 그가 한가운데를 차지하고 나는 가장자리로 밀려나 차문에 착 달라붙어 있잖아.

시장에 도착했을 때는 이미 둘 다 진이 빠졌어. 닭집 앞에서 다모는 곧 토할 것처럼 얼굴이 샛노래졌어. 바닥에 물이 흥건해서 앞사람들이 가지를 못하는데도, 다모는 그 털 뽑힌 닭무더기의 참상으로부터 빨리 벗어나려고 발을 동동 구르는 거야. 마침내 양손으로 바짓가랑이를 거머쥐고 까치발로 겅중겅중 뛰기 시작했어. 나는 코밑에서 탁구공처럼 오락가락하는 그의 머리통보다 한 팔쯤은 높이 눈을 두고 시장을 한 바퀴 둘러보았어. 보통 사람보다 훌쩍 키가 큰 무라뜨를 찾고 있지. 어쩌면 그도 고기를 사러 이 시장에 왔을지도 모르잖아. 이 도시에서 좋은 고기를 살 수 있는 곳은 몇 군데가 안 돼. 그가 여기 왔다면 곧 눈에 띄지 않을 수가 없어. 그는 어디서나 숙주나물 속에 낀 콩나물 한 줄기처럼 비죽 솟아나와 있지. 비록 이 나라에서 천대받는 하층민들보다도 검긴 하지만.

wears contacts, he has opts for glasses to protect himself on windy days like today. He claims that sandy winds can cause not only diseases of the respiratory organs but also eye and skin diseases as well as allergies.

He is agitated by the beggars who make threats and tug at your clothes instead of simply pleading, by the police officer who takes the trouble of crossing the street to inspect his ID. These, among many other reasons, upset him. Going out to buy a bottle of soy sauce is an adventure with too many twists and turns. When I'm by his side, I feel a kind of pressure that squeezes down on my lungs. I bet this is the feeling the divers mean when they speak of hydraulic pressure in deep water. Pushed by his inflamed rage, I find myself cowering. I cannot fathom how his temper is so fiery when he eats neither garlic nor onions nor ground chili pepper. Although we were seated evenly in the back of the taxi when we left, soon I was pushed to the far corner by that childlike, small and thin body of his, and now I'm pressed flat against the door of the cab.

When we get to the market, we're both already exhausted. In front of the poultry shop, Damo's face turns sallow, as if he were about to throw up.

사진첩을 가져다준 때가 마지막이었던 것 같아. 그 이후로 한 달도 넘게 무라뜨를 보지 못했어. 그가 아파서 오지 못하는 것만 아니라면 됐다고, 처음에 나는 그렇게 생각하려고 했어. 그러나 시간이 흐를수록 그게 아니야. 요즘은 새벽에 속이 쓰려 잠을 깨면 제일 먼저 무라뜨가 떠올라. 그에 대한 그리움은 속 쓰림만큼 예리하고 위통만큼 격렬해. 아니, 나는 배가 고프기 때문에 그가 미치도록 보고 싶은 거야.

무라뜨가 내 부엌을 필요로 하는 것보다 내가 더 절실히 그를 필요로 하는 줄 미처 몰랐어. 1, 2주일에 한 번씩 그가 포식하는 모습을 보면서 나 또한 그 덕분에 허기를 달랬던 거야. 내게는 내가 못 먹는 걸 대신 먹어줄 사람이 필요해. 먹고 싶은 대로 마음껏, 더 이상 먹을 수 없을 때까지, 이게 몸에 좋은가 나쁜가 따지지도 않고, 뭐든 삼갈 필요 없이, 꺼리지도 참지도 말고, 무지막지하게 먹어주는 사람. 음식을 놓고도 트릿하기만 한 다모 앞에서 내가 가슴이 미어지도록 느꼈던 안타까움은, 실은 타는 갈증, 환장할 듯한 허기였던 거야. 아, 배고파.

부엌에서 고기 굽는 연기가 나지 않고, 내 앞에서 게

The crowd is hardly moving because of the puddles on the floor. Damo trots impatiently in place, looking desperate to escape from the atrocious sight of the mass of chickens with their feathers all plucked. He eventually resorts to holding up his pant legs with his hands and jumping on his toes in long strides. I fix my gaze at a height about an arm's length above his head, which bobs up and down like a ping-pong ball under my nose. I take a look all around the market in search of Murat, who is a good foot taller than most people. Who knows, maybe he's also at this market to buy meat. There are few places in this city where you can get quality meat. If he's here, there is no way you can't spot him. He's always sticking out like a soybean sprout stem in a sea of mung bean sprouts, although he's darker than the basest class which is only treated with contempt.

The time he came over with the photo book must have been the last time. I haven't seen Murat since, for over a month. At first I just wanted to think that everything was okay unless he couldn't come over because he was sick. But the more time passes, the less that is the case. These days, Murat

걸스럽게 먹어대던 사람이 사라지자 내 굶주림은 흉포해졌어. 신문조차 읽을 수 없고 잠도 오지 않아. 앉지도 서지도 못하고 온종일 방 안을 맴돌아. 온몸이 텅 빈 듯한데 시도 때도 없이 울분이 휩쓸고 지나가. 얼마나 더 오래 이 형벌을 견뎌야 하느냐고, 들어줄 사람도 없는데 나는 항변해. 세상이 돌고 도는 법이라면 내가 받기만 하고 갚지 못한 은혜도, 어느 누구한테인가 저지른 잘못도 이제 나는 어떤 식으로든 갚지 않았느냐고.

무라뜨의 기숙사로 찾아가볼까도 했지만 종교단체에서 기증했다는 그 건물은 여자의 출입이 금지돼 있다고 했어. 전화는 경비실에 한 대뿐이라 걸 때마다 통화 중이고, 멀지도 않은 동네에 살면서 편지를 쓰기도 쑥스럽고. 설령 쓴다 해도 오지 않는 사람이 답장을 하겠는가 말이야. 혹시 그는 고기 요리를 맘껏 해 먹을 수 있는 다른 부엌을 찾아냈는지도 몰라. 그 생각을 할 때마다 나는 아찔해. 이 가공할 굶주림을 나더러 이제 어쩌라고.

짐꾼들이 다투어 앞길을 가로막고 눈이 마주치는 상인들마다 친구처럼 야단스럽게 알은척을 해. 파리를 쫓

is the first thing I think of when I awake at dawn from heartburn. The way I miss him is as acute as heartburn and as intense as a stomach pain. Well, no, I miss him like crazy because of my hunger.

I had no idea that I needed Murat more desperately than he needed my kitchen. I was satisfying my hunger by watching him stuff himself every week or two. I need someone to eat for me the things I cannot eat. As much as he wants, until he can eat no more. Not thinking about whether something is good or bad for you, with nothing off-limits. Someone to eat mercilessly without avoiding or holding back anything. The heart-rending pity I felt for a tepid Damo facing food was, in fact, a burning thirst, a maddening hunger. Oh, I'm starving.

My starvation has become brutal ever since my kitchen stopped smelling of grilled meat and the man who wolfed it down in front of me disappeared. I can't even read the newspaper or fall asleep. I can neither stand nor sit; I just pace in my room all day. My body feels completely empty, yet wrath rushes through it at all times of the day. How much longer must I endure this punishment, I protest, though I know no one can hear me. If the

으려고 생선가게에서 모기향을 피워놓아 좁은 통로가 자욱해. 치즈집에서는 김장독보다도 큰 양푼에 시큼한 우유를 끓이고 있어. 사람들이 간이식당 바깥까지 밀려 나와 선 채로 뭔가를 먹어대고 있어. 날것과 익은 것, 차가운 것과 뜨거운 것, 해산물과 견과, 향신료와 시든 야채, 온갖 종류의 음식물들이 뒤섞여, 비릿하면서도 달착지근하고 매캐하기도 한 냄새가 시장통에 차 있어.

나는 위경련이 시작될 조짐을 느꼈어. 어느새 겨드랑이가 흠뻑 젖었어. 겨울이 언제 지났는지도 모르겠는데 벌써 여름이야. 사막이 가까운 이 도시에는 봄이 없지. 겨울, 그리고 곧바로 여름. 그러고 보니 작년에 내가 이 도시에 도착했을 때 사람들은 조만간 닥칠 더위를 걱정하고 있었어. 이 시장에서만 판다는 찰기 있는 쌀을 사려고 내가 다모와 무라뜨를 따라 여기 처음 들렀던 게 꼭 이맘때였지. 이 1년 동안 또 우리가 서로에게 지운 사랑과 증오의 빚을 생각하면 나는 눈앞이 아찔해.

"뭐 해요? 이러다 서로 어긋나면 어쩌려고."

다모가 턱 밑에서 올려다보고 있어. 앞서 가다가 나를 데리러 온 모양이야. 보름 만에 그는 더욱 형편없이 졸아들었어. 고국 증권회사들의 돌발적인 도산으로 십몇

world goes round and round indeed, haven't I already paid back in whatever manner the favors given to me so far, as well as any transgressions committed against others?

I thought about going to Murat's dorm, but I understand women are forbidden at the building that was donated to them by a religious organization. The only phone there, at the front security desk, is busy whenever I call, yet it feels funny to send a letter to someone who lives nearby. And even if I were to write, would he write me back when he's not even coming to see me? Perhaps he has found another kitchen where he can cook meat to his heart's content. I go out of my mind whenever I think about that possibility. What am I to do with this terrifying hunger now?

Porters vie to block your way, and every merchant whose glance you meet makes a big fuss like a long-lost buddy. The narrow corridor is filled with the smoke from the mosquito-repellent sticks at the fish shop. At the cheese shop, they're boiling sour milk in a bucket bigger than a ceramic kimchi jar. People spilling out of the snack bar are all eating something standing up. Raw and cooked, cold

년 직장생활을 하면서 투자해놓았던 돈을 상당히 잃은 눈치야. 그는 도대체 상황이 어떻게 돼 가는지 알아보기 위해서라도 귀국해야 하지 않을까 고민하고 있어.

빨리 따라오라는 뜻으로 내게 눈을 한번 흘기고는 다모는 다시 바짓가랑이를 들어올리고 비틀거리며 인파를 빠져나갔어. 그게 내 눈에는 그가 허둥대며 도망가고 있는 것처럼 보여. 결코 피할 수 없는 고난, 빠져나갈 수 없는 불행, 거부해서는 안 되는 운명으로부터 달아나려는 헛된 몸부림만 같아. 나는 어린애의 손을 놓친 어머니처럼 가슴이 철렁해.

"내가 이럴 줄 알고 차에 타기 전에 요금부터 흥정해야 한다고 얘기했잖아요. 그랬으면 운전사가 알아서 가장 빠른 길로 갔을 텐데요."

장 본 짐을 택시에 싣고 출발한 지 얼마 되지도 않아 다모가 운전사의 뒤통수를 힐끔거리며 내게 속삭였어.

"전번에는 택시를 타면 운전사한테 미터기를 올리라고 요구하라고 그랬잖아요."

"그건 가까운 데 갈 때 이야기구요. 멀리 갈 때는 이 사람들이 똑같은 길을 세 바퀴 네 바퀴 뱅뱅 돌아도 여기 지리를 잘 모르는 우린 알아채지 못한다구요. 이런

and hot. Seafood and nuts. Spices and wilted vegetables. All kinds of food all mixed up. Smells at once fishy and sweet and spicy fill the marketplace.

I feel the sign of imminent stomach cramps. My armpits are completely soaked. Winter was seemingly just here, yet it's already summer. There's no spring in this city, close to the desert. Winter, then summer immediately. Come to think of it, when I arrived here last year people were concerned with the heat wave that would soon be coming. It was exactly around this time last year that Damo and Murat led me here, the only place around that sells sticky rice. Reflecting on all the baggage of love and hate we've created for one another over the past ycar, I shudder.

"What are you doing? We don't want to lose each other."

Damo is under my chin looking up at me. He must have doubled back to get me. He has shrunken even more abysmally over the last couple of weeks. I suspect the unexpected bankruptcy of investment firms in his home country caused him to lose a significant portion of the money he invested for over ten years. He's wondering whether he shouldn't go back home if only to find out how

얘기도 내가 다 했는데요, 왜. 내가 다 생각이 있어서 먼저 가격을 정하려는데 당신이 냉큼 택시에 올라탔으니 난들 어쩌겠어요."

"……"

"이러다 날은 깜깜해지구 만에 하나 이 친구가 마음을 잘못 먹어 우릴 어디 이상한 데로 끌고 가기라도 하면 어쩔 거냐구요. 엊그제 밤에 외국인 택시 승객한테 무슨 일이 있었는지, 신문 안 봤어요? 이거 아무래도 시간이 너무 걸리는 것 같단 말예요……"

다모의 두려움이 전해 와 나는 질식할 것만 같아. 그가 한평생 가슴에 키워온 공포는 나를 식빵조각처럼 단번에 짜부라뜨릴 듯해. 그러나 그가 한사코 도망치려는 대상이 애초부터 그러기가 불가능한, 막강한 것이라면 내가 할 수 있는 일이 뭐가 있겠어. 살기 위해 남에게 상처 주고, 남의 생명을 해치고, 남을 먹었으므로 언젠가는 상처를 받고, 생명을 빼앗기고, 먹힐 차례가 돌아오는 운명으로부터 그가 벗어나려고 발버둥친다면. 먹고 먹히는 생명의 법칙의 아가리에서 도망치려고 한다면.

부엌은 한증막처럼 김이 꽉 차 있어. 나는 뛰어가서

the situation is developing.

Damo gives me the evil eye as a sign that I should keep up with him, and staggers to navigate his way through the crowd, his hands again holding up his pant legs. It looks to me like an awkward and hurried escape. Like a vain struggle to run away from a fate you shouldn't deny, a misfortune you cannot dodge, or suffering you can never avoid. My heart jolts like that of a mother who's inadvertently let go of her child's hand.

"This is why I told you we should barter about the fare before we got into the car. Then the driver would have taken the fastest route possible."

Not long after we got our groceries and started on our way back in the taxi, Damo whispers this to me while glancing at the back of the driver's head.

"Didn't you tell me last time to wait until I got in the car to ask the driver to turn on the meter?"

"That's when you go a short distance. When it's a long trip, we can't tell if these people go in circles three, four times because we're not familiar with the streets around here. You know I've told you all this. I was going to get him to agree on the fare first for a reason but you just went ahead and got in the car, so what am I supposed to do?"

가스레인지부터 껐지. 얼마나 솥이 오래 끓고 있었는지 레인지 손잡이가 다 뜨겁고 타일벽에서도 열기가 느껴져. 솥뚜껑을 여니 수증기가 왈칵 달려들어. 나는 뒤로 물러나 김이 나가기를 기다렸다가 솥 안을 들여다보았지. 고깃덩어리가 그득해. 한 조각을 포크로 찔러보았어. 찔깃하지도 않고 폭, 예쁘게 구멍이 뚫려. 충분히 익었을 뿐만 아니라 고기가 연하다는 뜻이지. 덩어리가 큼지막해서 포크 하나로 들어올리기가 힘겨워. 비계가 많은 살집이 포크에서 쑥 빠져버릴 것만 같고, 그래서 위로 치켜들면 내 손등에까지 축축 늘어지니 어떻게 주체할 수가 없어. 사방에 소스가 튀고 말았네. 나는 검지 끝으로 식탁보에 찍힌 소스를 훑어 입에 넣고 쪽 빨았어. 그리고 막 떨어지려는 소스 방울을 혀로 받치면서 덥석 고깃덩어리를 물었지. 너무 뜨거워. 이가 얼얼하고 잇몸이 익어버리는 것 같아. 아, 얼마나 오랜만인가. 온몸의 세포가 국가대표팀을 응원하는 운동경기 관람객들처럼 일제히 함성을 지르며 일어서는 거야. 정수리와 발끝, 몸의 아래위에서 한꺼번에 심장이 북처럼 쾅쾅 울려. 나는 이빨에 지그시 힘을 주었어. 잠시 살코기와 내 이빨 사이에 긴장이 인다 싶었는데 싱겁게도 살

I don't answer.

"It'll get dark soon, and what if, a one in a million chance, this guy gets funny ideas and drags us to somewhere weird? Haven't you read in the paper what happened to a foreigner riding in a cab a couple of nights ago? This is taking way too long, I'm afraid—"

Damo's apprehension spreads and makes me feel suffocated. This fright, which he has nurtured in his heart his entire life, is about to squash me like a soft slice of bread. But what is there for me to do when the very object from which he's trying unrelentingly to flee is something with great power that can't be avoided from the get-go? If what he's struggling to escape is the fate, where in order to survive you hurt others and harm other lives, and then, as you've eaten someone, you are hurt, lose your life, and get your turn to be eaten at some point? What can you do if what you're trying to flee is the mouth of the eat-or-be-eaten law of life?

The kitchen is filled with steam like a sauna. I run over and turn off the stove. The pot has been boiling so long that even the knob for the gas feels hot and you can feel the heat coming from the tiled

덩어리가 뼈에서 쫙 뜯겼어. 뼈마디에 매달린 힘줄이 제법 고무줄처럼 늘어나다가 끊어져 내 입술을 찰싹 때리고는 입속으로 빨려 들어왔어. 누가 동물의 살을 단백질이라고 하는가, 그건 엄연히 지방, 젖처럼 꿀처럼 배어드는 액체인 것을. 그것은 고통, 꿀꺽 삼키면서 나는 신음까지 하지 않을 수가 없어.

그런데 왜 이 고기는 검은빛이 돌까, 눌었나? 질겅질겅 씹으면서 나는 손에 든 고깃덩이를 살펴보았어. 젤리처럼 반투명한 껍데기에 모근이 촘촘히 박혀 있고 케이크처럼 비계와 살이 층졌어. 껍질이 검다는 것 말고는 보통 고깃살하고 다를 게 없는데, 검정 살, 검은……

아! 무라뜨!

비로소 정신을 차리고 나는 솥 안을 주의 깊게 살펴보았어. 푹 익어서 흐물흐물해진 마늘과 양파 사이에서 무라뜨가 나를 훔쳐보고 있어. 쇠구슬처럼 또랑또랑한 그것이 다른 사람의 눈일 수가 없지. 반가운 마음에 나는 급히 수저를 찾아 들었어. 잘 익은 안구를 주위에 괸 찐득거리는 육즙과 함께 수저로 곱게 떠서 호로록 들이마셨어. 무라뜨의 눈동자가 천천히 식도를 타고 내려갔어. 나는 한동안 눈을 감고 내 속으로 깊이, 깊이 가라앉

backsplash. I open the pot cover only to be assaulted by more steam. Taking a step backward, I wait for the steam to disperse, and then look inside the pot. It is loaded with chunks of meat. I poke one with a fork. The meat isn't tough, and the fork easily makes nice holes. That tells me that the meat is at once fully cooked and tender. These are big chunks, and I barely manage to pick one up with the fork. The meat, heavy on fat, feels as though it would slip off the fork just like that, and hangs down almost into my hand when I lift it up. It's tricky to control. Of course, the sauce splatters everywhere. I sweep up the sauce on the tablecloth with the tip of my index finger and suck it up. Then, as I catch a falling drop of sauce with my outstretched tongue, I bite into the meat. It's too hot. It numbs my teeth and threatens to cook my gums. Oh, how long it's been! Every cell in my entire body stands up with a roar at the same time, like sports fans cheering a match of the national team. I feel my heart thumping like a drum in the crown of my head and at the tip of my toes, top to bottom, all at once. I slowly bite down with more force. There is a brief tension between the meat and my teeth, but insipidly, the chunk of meat is

는 무라뜨를 음미했어. 눈을 뜨자 얼핏 현기증마저 일어. 부엌 천장이 반 바퀴쯤 돌다가 멈췄어. 아까보다 더 허기가 져. 나는 다시 솥에 달려들었어. 활짝 핀 목화송이 같은 것이 눈길을 끌어. 이것 봐, 무라뜨의 머릿속이 이토록 화사한 줄 나는 알고 있었어! 나는 그의 골을 입에 담뿍 물었어. 뽀드득뽀드득, 입 안에서 첫눈 밟는 소리가 나.

이윽고 나는 수저통에서 기다란 젓가락을 뽑아 들었어. 솥 안을 이리저리 헤집었어. 돌돌 말린 내장에다 꺾인 뼈다귀, 신체 어느 부위인지 털이 숭숭 난 살덩어리까지 온갖 잡동사니가 그 안에 다 들어 있어. 내가 이제껏 살아오면서 알았던 모든 사람들, 내가 사랑하고 나를 사랑해주었던 사람들, 상처 받고 상처 주었던 사람들, 데면데면했던 사람들, 내가 실제로 본 적은 없는 유명인사들, 콘도르가 기다리는 앞에서 굶어 죽어가던 사진 속 아이, 옷깃 한 번 스친 인연밖에 없는 사람들, 옷깃도 한 번 안 스친 사람들, 이미 죽었으나 내게 알게 모르게 영향을 끼친 사람들, 그러지도 않은 죽은 자들, 살아도 나하고 만난 적 없고 만나지도 않을 절대다수, 죽을 사람들, 앞으로 살 사람들, 살지도 죽지도 않을 사람

soon torn away from the bone. The tendon on the bone stretches quite a bit like a rubber band before it snaps and slaps me on my lips as it is sucked into my mouth. Who called animal flesh protein, when it is indisputably fat, a seeping liquid like milk, like honey? It is torture: I can't help moaning as I swallow it with a gulp.

But why does this meat have a black hue? Was it scorched? Chewing on the meat like gum, I examine a chunk in my hand. Pores cover the jelly-like, semi-opaque skin, under which fat and flesh are layered like on a cake. This is an entirely ordinary piece of meat other than the fact that its skin is dark. Dark. Skin. Black—Oh! Murat!

Coming back to my senses only at this point, I look carefully into the pot. Between the garlic and the onion that are by now mushy from being cooked so long, Murat is peeping out at me. Those eyes, bright like metal balls, cannot belong to anyone else. Delightfully surprised, I grab a spoon. I gently scoop up a well-cooked eyeball along with the sticky gravy collected around it, and slurp it up. Murat's eye slowly goes down my esophagus. For a good while, I close my eyes and savor Murat as he sinks deeper and deeper inside me. When I open

들, 모두모두 공평한 고기토막이 되어 다 들어 있어. 크지도 작지도 않은 얄팍한 알루미늄 솥 안에 몽땅 모여 있어. 참으로 감격스럽고 고마운 일이야.

젓가락이 뭔가에 걸렸어. 뭔가 젓가락을 잡고 놓지를 않아. 나는 솥 가장자리에 몸을 의지하고 팔에 힘을 주었어. 불쑥 다른 고깃덩어리들을 헤치고 젓가락에 매달려 나오는 건 손이야. 뭔가 움켜쥐려는 듯이 갈퀴처럼 곱아버린 다모의 오른손이야. 별로 먹음직스럽지는 않지만, 내가 먹어주지 않는다면 다모는 또 화를 내겠지. 그나마 쫄깃한 힘줄이 씹을 만은 해. 나는 다모의 손마디를 톡톡 분질러서 마디에 덧씌운 물렁뼈를 병뚜껑 따듯 이빨로 벗겨냈어. 그리고 오도독오도독 씹었어. 뼈를 한 접시나 뱉어냈는데도 도무지 먹은 것 같지가 않아. 다시 젓가락을 들고 나는 솥 안을 노려보았어. 주먹만하게 오므라든, 자주색 심장에 눈이 멎었어. 나는 그걸 젓가락으로 찍었어. 그런데 다모가 그 심장을 평생 얼마나 조이고 조였으면 젓가락이 들어가지를 않아. 숟가락으로 떠내려 해도 약 올리려는 듯이 덱데굴 굴러 떨어지고 말아. 도리 없이 나는 두 손으로 그걸 솥에서 들어내어 여기저기 깨물어보았어. 너무 쫀쫀해서 도무

my eyes, I'm even a bit dizzy. The kitchen ceiling spins halfway before stopping. I'm hungrier than before. I pounce on the pot again. Something that looks like a cotton flower in full bloom catches my eye. Look here! I always knew inside Murat's head was this resplendent! I take a mouthful of his brain. *Squish, squish.* In my mouth it makes sound like walking on new snow.

Soon I pull out a pair of extra-long chopsticks from the drawer. I rummage through the pot. From a coiled-up piece of innards to a bent bone to a chunk of hairy flesh from some part of the body, all kinds of odds and ends are in it. All of the people I have known in my life; those I have loved and those who have loved me; those I have hurt and those who have hurt me; those people who could take me or leave me and vice versa; those famous people whom I have never met in person; the kid in a photo I saw, dying of starvation in front of a waiting condor; those people with whom I've only once come in contact;[2)] those who have not once come in contact with me; those who are long dead but have nonetheless influenced me in ways obvious and not so obvious; those dead who have never influenced me; the overwhelming majority of

지 씹히지를 않아. 내가 이빨에 힘을 줄 때마다 어느 구멍에선가 국물이 찔끔대며 새나와, 내 손목을 나선형으로 감으며 흘러내릴 뿐이야. 나는 소매를 걷고 그 찔끔거리는 구멍에 입을 대고 빨아보았어. 미지근한 국물이 입에 가득 고여. 밍밍하고 비릿해. 나는 꿀꺽 삼켰어.

열대의 더위가 시작되리라는 조짐이야. 만나는 사람들마다 밤잠을 설치고 두통에 시달린다는 하소연이야. 무라뜨는 다른 때보다 배나 많은 음식을 만들어놓고는, 평소만큼도 못 먹고 땀만 엄청나게 흘리고 있어.

"무라뜨!"

"……"

내가 몇 번이나 불렀건만 그는 대답하지 않아.

"무라뜨!"

"……"

능글맞은 웃음기마저도 오늘은 없어. 꾸중이라도 들은 것처럼 숙인 얼굴은 뺨이 더욱 패였어. 세상만사 겪을 만큼 겪은 중년처럼 보이긴 해도 10년 전쯤 아라비아 해를 건널 때 열몇 살이었다니, 그는 아직도 20대야. 입만 열면 음담패설을 쏟아놓지만 실제로는 그는 몹시

those living whom I have neither met nor shall ever meet; those who will die; those who will be alive in the future; and those who will neither live nor die: all of them are in it as equal chunks of meat. They are here together in a thin aluminum pot that is not too big and not too small. I'm so touched and grateful.

My chopsticks catch on something. Something has grabbed on to them and will not let go. I anchor myself on the edge of the pot and yank harder. Abruptly, it comes out, hanging on the chopsticks and pushing aside other chunks of meat. It's a hand. Hooked like a rake, as if intending to clutch at something: it's Damo's right hand. Although it does not look terribly appetizing, if I don't eat it, Damo will get mad at me again. At least the chewy tendons make it worth my while. I break Damo's fingers and strip off with my teeth the cartilages covering the knuckles, like removing a bottle cap. Then I crunch and chew them. I spit out a plateful of bones, yet I hardly feel I have eaten anything. Picking up the chopsticks again, I stare back into the pot. My eyes stop at the purple-colored heart shrunken to the size of a fist. I stab it with my chopsticks. But they won't go in, apparently be-

수줍음을 타는군. 나는 잠자코 일어나 옷을 벗었어.

건성으로 고깃덩이만 뒤적이던 무라뜨가 힘없이 포크를 내려놓았어. 나는 접시를 구석으로 밀어내고 식탁에 누워, 순한 양처럼 목을 길게 늘어뜨렸어. 그의 목에 불거진 목울대가 단번에 위로 올라갔다가 미끄러져 내렸어.

"나를 먹어요!"

나는 속삭였어. 다모에게 그랬듯이 나는 무라뜨에게 내 부엌문을 활짝 열었어. 무라뜨가 몸서리를 쳤어. 내가 다모를 먹었듯이, 그는 나를 먹기 시작했어. 잉잉잉, 벽 속에서 수도관이 울어. 집집마다 늦은 저녁밥을 짓느라고 분주해. 찬장문을 여닫고 도마질하는 소리가 요란해. 스테인리스 접시들이 쨍강거리고 칙칙칙, 압력밥솥이 경쟁적으로 끓고 있어. 새벽부터 한밤까지 사람들은 부엌에서 뭔가를 씻고, 끓이고, 튀기고 있어. 나는 음식, 음식, 음식이 되었어.

『부엌』, 강, 2006

cause Damo wrung that heart of his so hard all his life. When I go at it with a spoon, it rolls off as if to mock me. Left with no other choice, I pick it up with my hands and try biting into a few spots here and there. It's so dense that I can hardly get my teeth through it. Every time I press with my teeth, juice seeps out from a hole somewhere, running down my wrists in a spiral. I push up my sleeves, put my mouth over a leaking hole, and suck on it. My mouth is filled with lukewarm juice. It's bland and a bit fishy. I gulp it down.

There are signs that tropical heat is about to start. Everyone you meet bemoans sleep trouble and headaches. Murat has made double the normal amount of food, yet all he's doing is sweat buckets while eating less than his usual portion.

"Murat!"

I keep calling him, but he doesn't respond.

"Murat!"

The characteristic sly smile is absent today. His head is down as if he'd just been yelled at, and his cheeks have become even gaunter. Although he may look like a middle-aged man who's been though it all, he crossed the Arabian Sea as a teenager ten or so years ago, which only makes him in his twenties still. Hmm, in spite of all the non-stop dirty jokes that pour out of his mouth, he's actually quite shy. I get up without a word and get undressed.

Murat, who's been mindlessly fiddling with pieces of meat, puts down his fork lethargically. I push the plates to the edge and lie across on the table, stretching down my neck like a docile lamb. His protruding Adam's apple goes up then slides down in an instant.

"Eat me!" I whisper.

As I did for Damo, I open wide the door to my kitchen for Murat. A shiver runs through Murat's body. As I ate Damo, Murat begins to eat me. The water pipe whimpers inside the wall. Every home is busy preparing dinner. There are loud noises of cupboard doors opening and closing, of chopping on cutting boards. Stainless steel plates are clanging, and pressure cookers are hissing and screeching in competition. From dawn to midnight, people are in the kitchen washing, boiling, and frying something. And I have become food, food, food.

1) Joseph Campbell, *The Mystic Image*. Princeton University Press, 1974, pp. 126-129. (This is the author's own footnote. -tr.)

2) The original text, translatable as "those people whose clothes have only once come in contact with mine," is a reference to a well-known Buddhist-inspired saying. It means that anyone with whom you have the slightest contact has a fateful connection to you that was formed over a very long series of previous lifetimes. In contemporary popular culture, this saying is used to add significance to events that are apparently accidental or random.

Translated by Chris Choi

해설

Afterword

먹는 것이 고통인 세상에서 벗어나는 길

이현식 (문학평론가)

오수연은 한국문학의 영토와 상상력을 넓혀온 작가이다. 한국문학은 그동안 민족과 국가의 영역 안에 강하게 갇혀왔다. 예외가 없었던 것은 아니지만 한국문학이 그려왔던 대상은 우리민족과 관련된 범주를 많이 넘어서지 못했던 것이 사실이다. 그러나 오수연의 「나는 음식이다」는 그 틀을 사뿐히 넘어서고 있다. 이 소설의 공간은 한국이 아닌 동양의 어떤 나라이다. 그 나라가 정확히 어느 곳인지는 알 수 없다. 작가가 작품 발표 전에 인도에 2년간 머물렀다는 점에서 인도라고 추정할 수 있을 뿐, 그곳이 인도라고 단정할 명시적 정보는 작품 안에서 찾기 힘들다. 등장인물 역시 마찬가지이다.

The Way Out of the World Where Eating Is Suffering

Lee Hyeon-sik (literary critic)

Oh Soo-yeon is a writer who has expanded the imagination and territory of Korean literature, which had until only recently been solidly confined to the domain of the Korean people and state. While there have been exceptions, it is nonetheless true that the subjects of Korean literature have rarely left the realms of the Korean people. Oh Soo-yeon's "I Am Food," however, steps out of that frame with ease. The space within this story is not Korea but a country in Asia. We do not know exactly where it is. While one can surmise that it is India based on the fact that the author stayed there for two years preceding the publication of the story, there is little, if any, explicit information in the

작중화자인 '나'는 분명 한국인이지만 함께 등장하는 '다모'와 '무라뜨'는 어느 나라 사람들인지 알 수 없다. 그들도 작품의 배경이 된 나라에서 '나'와 다를 바 없이 이방인이고 동양의 어느 곳, 아프리카의 어느 곳 출신이라는 것만 막연히 추측할 수 있을 뿐이다. 그렇게 본다면 「나는 음식이다」에서 작가는 작품의 배경이 되는 국가나 등장인물들의 민족적 정체성은 중요한 게 아니라고 생각하고 있는 것이 분명하다. 그렇다 보니 작가의 상상력은 더 이상 한국에서의 삶이나 우리 민족이 당면한 문제 같은 것에 갇혀 있지 않다.

대신 작가는 사람이 살아가는 그 자체가 중요한 것이라고 생각하는 것 같다. 그런데 대체 살아가는 것이란 무엇인가? 작가는 이 작품의 제목이 상징하듯이 산다는 것은 바로 먹는 것이고 먹는 문제야말로 삶의 문제에 가장 앞자리에 선다는 것을 드러내 보여준다. 「나는 음식이다」에서 사람의 차이를 가르는 문제가 바로 먹는 문제로 드러나고 있기 때문이다. 작중화자가 살고 있는 동네의 사원 앞에 내걸린 걸신들린 '신'의 모습은 그것을 상징한다. 그런데 여기에서 '먹는' 문제는 일종의 은유로도 읽을 수 있다. 자기의 욕망을 채우는 행위가 '먹

work from which one can conclude this with certainty. This is also the case with the characters. The narrator is definitely Korean, but the nationalities of "Damo" and "Murat," the characters who appear alongside the narrator, are unclear. One can merely speculate that they are, as is the narrator, foreigners to the country that is the backdrop of the story, and that they come from somewhere in Asia and in Africa, respectively. From this, it becomes clear that the author does not consider important the exact name of the country or the national identity of the characters. And it naturally follows that the author's imagination is no longer bound by such factors as life within Korea or problems facing the Korean people.

Instead, the author seems to deem important the act of living itself. But what, exactly, is living? As symbolized by the story's title, the author demonstrates that living is eating, and that eating is at the forefront of life's issues. For what determines the difference among people in "I Am Food" manifests itself as the issue with eating. Its symbol is the figure of the eating-demon-possessed "god" hanging on the front of the temple in the neighborhood where the narrator is living. Of course, the issue of

는다'는 행위 일반으로도 해석될 수 있는 것이다.

그것이 '영광의 얼굴'이라고 사람들이 말했어. 먹을 게 없으니까 자신의 사지를 먹어치우고 머리통만 남은 괴물이라고. 도저히 채워질 수 없는 가공할 굶주림으로 어떤 악마건 삼켜버리기 때문에 사원을 수호한다고 했어. 동굴처럼 벌어진 그 입이.

이 소설에서는 사람들이 무엇을 먹는가가 바로 그 사람을 드러내는 정체성이다. 채식주의자인 '다모'와 육식을 탐닉하는 '무라뜨'는 그들이 먹는 음식에 의해 구분되고 있기 때문이다. 그렇지만 채식주의자와 육식주의자가 무슨 우화처럼 대비되고 있는 것은 아니다. 사는 문제란 그렇게 간단한 문제가 아닌 것 또한 사실이다. 채식주의자이지만 날카롭고 까다로운 성격의 소유자가 '다모'이고 육식주의자이면서도 공격적이기보다는 무던한 사람 됨됨이를 보여주는 게 '무라뜨'인 것이다. '다모'는 채식주의자라기보다 음식 혐오주의자에 가까운 모습을 보이기도 한다. 이 둘은 이 작품에서 서로 마주치지 않는다. 먹는 게 다르니 마주칠 이유가 없는 것

"eating" here can also be read as a kind of metaphor. An act of fulfilling one's desires can be interpreted as the general act of "eating."

People told me it is the "face of glory." They said it's a monster who's devoured his own body save for his head, because there was nothing else to eat. Thanks to its formidable, ravenous, and insatiable appetite, it protects the temple by swallowing any and all demons. It protects the temple with its mouth that's open like a cave.

In this work, what people eat is the very identity that defines them. The vegetarian Damo and the meat-indulging Murat are distinguished by the food they eat. But the contrast between the vegetarian and the carnivore is unlike that in a fable. After all, the matter of living is not so simple. Damo has a sharp, difficult personality although he is a vegetarian, and Murat, while carnivorous, displays an easygoing, rather than aggressive, temperament. Damo is sometimes closer to being a hater of food than a vegetarian. These two characters do not meet in the story. There is no reason for them to meet because what they eat is different.

이다.

그런데 이 작품의 무게중심은 '무라뜨'보다는 '다모'에게 다가가 있다. 먹는 행위란 결국 남에게 상처를 주고 생명을 빼앗는 행위라는 '다모'의 음식 혐오증을 작가는 세심하게 파고들고 있다. 그렇지만 「나는 음식이다」에서는 오히려 그런 생각이 타인에게 상처를 주는 것으로 그려지고 있다. '다모'의 음식 혐오증 때문에 상처받는 사람이 바로 '나'이고 '나'는 '다모'로 인해 고통을 받는다. 아이러니컬하게도 생명을 존중하고 타인에게 상처주지 않겠다는 '다모'의 생각이 오히려 '다모'에게 음식을 조금이라도 먹이려는 '나'의 배려를 무시하고 '나'를 고통스럽게 만드는 요인인 것이다.

작품 끝부분에서 '무라뜨'도 먹어치우고 '다모'까지 먹어버리는, 마침내 화자인 '나' 스스로도 남에게 먹힐 수 있는 존재인 음식으로 바뀌어 '무라뜨'에게 "나를 먹어요!"라고 속삭이는 환상적이고도 그로테스크한 장면은 먹는 고통에서 벗어나려는 '나'의 몸부림이기도 하다. 먹고 먹히는 세상, 먹는 것을 즐거움으로 삼건 고통으로 여기건 먹는 것 때문에 힘들어 하는 세상에서 '나'는 스스로 음식이 됨으로써 그 고통의 쇠사슬로부터 벗어

But this story is centered more on Damo than Murat. The author scrupulously explores Damo's hatred of food, which asserts that the act of eating is ultimately an act of hurting others and taking away lives. But in the portrayal of "I Am Food" it is this sort of belief that ends up hurting others. Damo's hatred of food hurts the narrator; the narrator must continually suffer because of Damo. Ironically, Damo's intention of respecting all lives and not hurting others leads him to neglect the considerateness of the narrator, who wants to feed Damo even a little; it also causes her to suffer.

There's a scene, at once fantastic and grotesque, that comes toward the end of the piece when the narrator has eaten Murat and Damo: the narrator becomes food as well. Finally, she wants to be eaten by others, and she whispers, "Eat me!" to Murat. It is also the narrator's struggle to escape the pain of eating. In the eat-and-be-eaten world where eating leads to trouble regardless of whether one considers it joy or suffering, the narrator attempts to flee from that suffering by becoming food herself. Ultimately, "I Am Food" demonstrates in a roundabout way how to overcome the difficulties of human life through the process of self-deliver-

나려 하는 것이다. 결국 「나는 음식이다」는 주인공 스스로가 음식이 되는 자기 해탈의 과정을 통해 사람살이의 힘겨움을 어떻게 극복할 수 있는지를 우회적으로 보여주고 있는 것이다.

ance by the protagonist's becoming food herself.

비평의 목소리

Critical Acclaim

오수연은 기록했다. 오수연은 중동 한복판에서 공포에 질린 팔레스타인과 이라크 민중들의 비극적 육성을 기록했다. 이는 신선한 충격이며 획기적인 사건이다. 식민통치와 군부독재, 남북대립으로 요약되는 한국현대사의 전개과정에서 한국 문인들은 아주 자연스럽게 문학적 시선을 한반도 내로 제한할 수밖에 없었다. 그러나 오수연을 통해 그 시선은 국가와 민족의 경계를 뛰어넘어 국제적 연대를 구체적으로 모색하고 수행하는 전지구적 당대성을 획득한다. 오수연은 국가와 민족의 범주를 이탈하되 그 이탈의 종착지는 국제주의적 연대라는 걸 보여주고 있으니, 그의 언어와 육성은 문학

Oh Soo-yeon is a recorder. Oh recorded the tragic voices of frightened Palestinian and Iraqi masses from the very center of the Middle East. This was a refreshing jolt and a landmark event. In the course of modern Korean history that can be summed up through the events of Japanese colonization, military dictatorship, and conflict between the North and the South, Korean writers naturally limited their artistic gaze to the Korean peninsula. But through Oh, that gaze has transcended national and racial confines and has obtained a global contemporaneity that searches for and carries out international fellowship. While Oh dissociates herself

의 보편적 가치로 오랜 시간 회자되었으나, 그 실질적 의미를 잃은 인권, 자유, 평등 등등을 당대적 의미를 획득한 구체적 표현으로 부활시키고 있다.

양진오

폐쇄적, 개인적, 환상적 통과제의로서의 『부엌』. 미궁으로부터의 영웅적 탈출이 아니라 미궁의 고통 속에 끝내 남겨지는 것, 이것이 오히려 현대적 통과제의의 정직한 윤리인지도 모른다. 본래 통과제의는 신참자들에게만 해당되는 것이 아니라 집단 전체에 해당되는 기강 확립의 시도이다. 그런데 『부엌』은 이런 공공성·집단성이 거세된 통과제의이며 공동체의 기강 확립이 아니라 공동체 자체에 저항하는 형태의 '반사회성'을 띤 통과제의라는 점에서 주목된다. 그녀의 통과제의와 전통적 통과제의의 결정적인 차이는 그 목적이 전통적 공동체로의 '귀환(귀속)'이 아니라 주어진 세계의 폭력에 대한 '저항'이라는 점이다. 그녀의 통과제의는 세계의 폭력을 대속하고, 세계의 폭력에 저항하는 것이다. '부엌'을 진지로 삼은 그들의 통과제의는 어쩌면 누군가가 굶어 죽는 상황이 멈추지 않는 한, 누군가의 살을 먹어 살아남아

from the category of the state and ethnicity, she has shown that the ultimate destination of this dissociation is global fellowship. Her language and voice revive such concepts as human rights, freedom, and equality, which, despite being addressed as general literary values for a long time, lost their practical significance as specific expressions with contemporary significance.

Yang Jin-o

The Kitchen is a closed, private, and fantastic rite of passage; remaining in the pain within the labyrinth, rather than escaping heroically from this labyrinth, may be the honest ethics of a modern rite of passage. A rite of passage is, at its core, an attempt to establish an order that applies not only to new members but also to an entire group. Yet *The Kitchen* is notable for being a rite of passage devoid of such public and collective elements, an "antisocial" one that rejects the concept of community itself rather than establishes communal order. The decisive difference between her rite of passage and a traditional one is that the objective of hers is not a "return (reversion)" to traditional community but a "rebellion" against the violence of the given world.

야 하는 생명의 사슬이 끝나지 않는 한, 끝나지 않을 것이다.

정여울

생경한 구호가 되기 쉬운 정치적 올바름의 문제는, 그의 소설 속에서 실은 정치적이라기보다 윤리적인 것에 가깝다. 작가는 점령군과 독재자, 혹은 미국과 팔레스타인의 대립을 부각시키는 것이 아니라, 그 속에서 개개인의 삶은 어떻게 파괴되어가는 것인지에 궁극적인 관심을 두고 있다. 이를테면 평화를 내세우는 국제적 연대, 구호 단체의 내부에도 얼마나 다양한 이해관계가 존재하고, 얼마나 많은 위선이 존재하는지, 그리고 그들 역시 얼마나 허약한 존재들인지에 대해 가감 없이 보여주고 있다. 한편, 외부에서 강제되는 상황에 속수무책으로 삶을 내맡길 수밖에 없고, 주체적으로 자기 삶의 주인이 될 수 없으며, 최소한의 인간다움을 보장받을 수 없는 사람들의 비극적 이야기는 우리의 머리와 가슴으로 직핍한다. 즉 오수연 소설의 정치적 올바름은 거창한 슬로건이나 당위에서 출발하기 이전에, 바로 “누구도 이렇게 살 수는 없어”라는 인간의 가장 본능적

Her right of passage atones for, and rebels against, the violence of the world. Perhaps the rite of passage of those stationed in the kitchen will not be complete until no more die from starvation, unless the chain of life, where in order to survive one must eat another's flesh, comes to an end.

Jeong Yeo-ul

The matter of political correctness, which runs the danger of becoming a stiff slogan, actually manifests itself in her work more along the lines of ethics rather than politics. Instead of focusing on the conflicts between occupying forces and a dictator, or between the U.S. and Palestine, the author locates her ultimate interest in how individual lives are destroyed within these conflicts. She is decisive in demonstrating how many conflicts of interest, as well as how much hypocrisy, exist within these international associations and humanitarian organizations even as they herald peace, and how fragile these associations and organizations are. Moreover, the tragic stories of those who have no choice but let externally imposed situations run their lives, who cannot take the agency of their own lives, and who are not assured of the smallest degree of hu-

인 절규와 기본적 권리에 대한 믿음에서 출발하고 있는 것이다.

김미정

인도에서 돌아온 그녀가 내놓은 『부엌』은 달랐다. 그것은 그녀 안에 잠복해 있던 '탈중심성'을 전면화시킨 작품집이었다. 그녀의 문장은 아름답지도 부드럽지도 않았기에 미문(美文)에 길들여진 모모한 비평가들을 당혹스럽게 했지만 그것은 분명 개성적인 문체였다. 이야기를 풀어가는 방식은 마치 서투른 작가의 그것처럼 보였지만 기실은 새로운 문제의식을 담아내려는 고민의 산물이었다. 그러한 새로움은 둔한 사람의 눈에는 뜨이지 않는 법이다. 그리하여 『부엌』은 국적성을 벗어나 인간의 존재방식을 묻는 세계시민의 소설로 한국문단에 출현했다.

방민호

maneness, speak directly to our minds and hearts. In other words, the political correctness in Oh Soo-yeon's fiction begins from humanity's most instinctual cry—"No one should have to live like this"—and from a faith in fundamental human rights, before it comes from grandiose slogans or rationales.

Kim Mi-jeong

The Kitchen, the book she published after returning from India, was something different. It was a collection of stories that brought to the surface the "de-centrality" that had been latent within her. Her writing, neither beautiful nor gentle, and confounding to those critics accustomed to flowery prose, nonetheless had its own style. Her way of unfolding her story may have resembled that of an unskilled writer, when it was, in fact, the product of a deliberate attempt to encompass a new critical approach. Such freshness is rarely discernible to an unperceptive reader. Thus, *The Kitchen* made its appearance in the Korean literary scene as a work of fiction that posed questions on the human way to be, transcending nationality into the realm of global citizenship.

Bang Min-ho

오수연

오수연은 1964년 서울에서 태어나 서울대학교 국어국문학과를 졸업했다. 1994년 《현대문학》 장편 공모에 『난쟁이 나라의 국경일』이 당선되어 소설을 쓰기 시작했다. 1997년 첫 작품집 『빈집』을 펴냈다. 이후 2년간 인도에 머물렀고, 이때의 경험은 연작 장편 『부엌』의 모태가 되었다. 『부엌』은 한국 유학생이 외국에서 음식을 통해 인간의 삶의 문제를 새로운 방식으로 고찰한 소설집이다. 2001년 『부엌』에 수록된 중편 「땅 위의 영광」으로 제34회 한국일보문학상을 수상했다. 2003년 '한국작가회의'의 이라크전쟁 파견 작가이자 한국이라크 반전평화팀 일원으로 이라크와 팔레스타인에 다녀왔다. 자원하여 이라크 전쟁터로 가는 것에 대해 당시 작가는 "미국의 전횡을 TV로 보고만 있기에는 너무 답답했고, 전쟁의 참상을 기록할 필요를 느꼈다"고 말했다.

2004년 이라크와 팔레스타인에 머물렀던 4개월간의 경험을 르포 형식의 문집 『아부 알리, 죽지 마—이라크 전쟁의 기록』에 담았다. 이 문집에서 작가는 이라크전

Oh Soo-yeon

Born in Seoul in 1964, Oh Soo-yeon graduated from the Department of Korean Literature of Seoul National University. She began writing fiction in 1994 when her *National Holiday in the Land of Dwarves* won in the novel category of *Hyundae Munhak*'s annual literary contest. *Vacant House*, her first collection of stories, was published in 1997. She stayed in India for two years after this, the experience from which time served as the matrix of *The Kitchen*, a collection of serialized stories. *The Kitchen* chronicles the novel exploration of human life by a student from Korea through the medium of food. Oh received the 2001 *Hankook Ilbo* Literary Award for the novella "Glory on Earth" from this volume of short stories. She spent time in Iraq and Palestine in 2003 as a dispatched Iraq-War representative for the Writers Association of Korea, and as a member of the Solidarity for Iraq Peace Team of Korea. On volunteering to participate in the Iraq War, Oh said at the time: "I was too restless to sit still and deplore U.S. despotism. I wanted to wit-

쟁의 과정에서 만난 다양한 계층의 사람들에 대한 이야기를 통해 전쟁이 인류의 가장 치밀한 범죄이며 비폭력은 무저항이 아니라 목숨을 건 투쟁이라는 점을 말하고 있다. 2006년에는 팔레스타인 현대 산문 선집 『팔레스타인의 눈물』을, 2008년에 팔레스타인과 한국 문인들의 칼럼 교환집 『팔레스타인과 한국의 대화』를 기획·번역하여 펴냈다. 2006년에는 '팔레스타인을 잇는 다리'라는 모임을 만들어 주도적으로 활동했다. 이 모임은 팔레스타인 가자지구 돕기 운동, 팔레스타인에서 한국영화 상영회 개최, 한국·팔레스타인 합동 전시회 개최 등의 성과를 올리고 2010년 해산하였다. 2007년에 연작소설 『황금지붕』을, 2011년에는 장편소설 『돌의 말』을 냈다. 한국작가회의 자유실천위원장, 국제위원장 등을 지냈다. 2006년에 제5회 아름다운 작가상, 2008년에 제26회 신동엽문학상을 각각 받았다.

ness the site of unfolding history as a writer."

In 2004, she incorporated her experience during her four months in Iraq and Palestine in *Don't Die, Abu Ali: The Chronicles of the Iraq War*, a collection of writing in the style of reportage. Through this collection's stories about people from the various classes she met during the Iraq War, Oh conveys that war is the most elaborate crime of humanity, and that nonviolence is not nonresistance but a struggle at the risk of one's life. Oh conceived, translated and published *Tears of Palestine*, a collection of contemporary Palestinian prose, in 2006, and *Palestine and Korea: A Dialogue,* a collection of exchange of columns by Palestinian and Korean writers, in 2008. She was an active founding member of the group "Bridge to Palestine" in 2006. This group had a number of accomplishments, including a movement to aid the Gaza section of Palestine, holding Korean film screenings in Palestine, and putting on a joint exhibition of Korean and Palestine art, before it disbanded in 2010. She published *The Golden Roof*, another collection of serialized stories, in 2007, and the novel *The Words from the Rock* in 2011. For the Writers Association of Korea, she has served as Chair of the Committee for Practical Freedom and Chair of International Committee. Oh won the Beautiful Artist award in 2006, and the Shin Dong-yeop Award for Literature in 2008.

번역 **크리스 최** Translated by Chris Choi

인문학자, 문화언어 컨설턴트. 매사추세츠 공대와 하버드에서 비교문학 박사 포함 총 네 개의 학위를 받았으며, 현재 뉴욕에 있는 컨설팅 펌 Educhora와 비영리단체인 Educhora Culture의 디렉터이다.

Chris Choi is apparently into balance. Bicultural and bilingual, she earned two degrees from M.I.T., then two more at Harvard, her final one a doctorate in Comparative Literature. As Director of Educhora, she researches, consults and facilitates learning on linguistic and cultural interaction, transition, fluency and impact. In addition to also directing the non-profit Educhora Culture, she spends time enjoying sports and fashion.

감수 **전승희, 데이비드 윌리엄 홍**

Edited by Jeon Seung-hee and David William Hong

전승희는 서울대학교와 하버드대학교에서 영문학과 비교문학으로 박사 학위를 받았으며, 현재 하버드대학교 한국학 연구소의 연구원으로 재직하며 아시아 문예 계간지 《ASIA》 편집위원으로 활동 중이다. 현대 한국문학 및 세계문학을 다룬 논문을 다수 발표했으며, 바흐친의 『장편소설과 민중언어』, 제인 오스틴의 『오만과 편견』 등을 공역했다. 1988년 한국여성연구소의 창립과 《여성과 사회》의 창간에 참여했고, 2002년부터 보스턴 지역 피학대 여성을 위한 단체인 '트랜지션하우스' 운영에 참여해 왔다. 2006년 하버드대학교 한국학 연구소에서 '한국 현대사와 기억'을 주제로 한 워크숍을 주관했다.

Jeon Seung-hee is a member of the Editorial Board of ***ASIA***, and a Fellow at the Korea Institute, Harvard University. She received a Ph.D. in English Literature from Seoul National University and a Ph.D. in Comparative Literature from Harvard University. She has presented and published numerous papers on modern Korean and world literature. She is also a co-translator of Mikhail Bakhtin's ***Novel and the People's Culture*** and Jane Austen's ***Pride and Prejudice***. She is a founding member of the Korean Women's Studies Institute and of the biannual Women's Studies' journal ***Women and Society*** (1988), and she has been working at 'Transition House,' the first and oldest shelter for battered women in New England. She organized a workshop entitled "The Politics of Memory in Modern Korea" at the Korea Institute, Harvard University, in 2006. She also served as an advising committee member for the Asia-Africa Literature Festival in 2007 and for the

POSCO Asian Literature Forum in 2008.

데이비드 윌리엄 홍은 미국 일리노이주 시카고에서 태어났다. 일리노이대학교에서 영문학을, 뉴욕대학교에서 영어교육을 공부했다. 지난 2년간 서울에 거주하면서 처음으로 한국인과 아시아계 미국인 문학에 깊이 몰두할 기회를 가졌다. 현재 뉴욕에서 거주하며 강의와 저술 활동을 한다.

David William Hong was born in 1986 in Chicago, Illinois. He studied English Literature at the University of Illinois and English Education at New York University. For the past two years, he lived in Seoul, South Korea, where he was able to immerse himself in Korean and Asian-American literature for the first time. Currently, he lives in New York City, teaching and writing.

바이링궐 에디션 한국 대표 소설 066

나는 음식이다

2014년 6월 6일 초판 1쇄 인쇄 | 2014년 6월 13일 초판 1쇄 발행

지은이 오수연 | **옮긴이** 크리스 최 | **펴낸이** 김재범
감수 전승희, 데이비드 윌리엄 홍 | **기획** 정은경, 전성태, 이경재
편집 정수인, 이은혜 | **관리** 박신영 | **디자인** 이춘희
펴낸곳 (주)아시아 | **출판등록** 2006년 1월 27일 제406-2006-000004호
주소 서울특별시 동작구 서달로 161-1(흑석동 100-16)
전화 02.821.5055 | **팩스** 02.821.5057 | **홈페이지** www.bookasia.org
ISBN 979-11-5662-018-1 (set) | 979-11-5662-038-9 (04810)
값은 뒤표지에 있습니다.

Bi-lingual Edition Modern Korean Literature 066

I Am Food

Written by Oh Soo-yeon | **Translated by** Chris Choi
Published by Asia Publishers | 161-1, Seodal-ro, Dongjak-gu, Seoul, Korea
Homepage Address www.bookasia.org | **Tel**. (822).821.5055 | **Fax**. (822).821.5057
First published in Korea by Asia Publishers 2014
ISBN 979-11-5662-018-1 (set) | 979-11-5662-038-9 (04810)

〈바이링궐 에디션 한국 대표 소설〉 작품 목록(1~60)

아시아는 지난 반세기 동안 한국에서 나온 가장 중요하고 첨예한 문제의식을 가진 작가들의 작품들을 선별하여 총 105권의 시리즈를 기획하였다. 하버드 한국학 연구원 및 세계 각국의 우수한 번역진들이 참여하여 외국인들이 읽어도 어색함이 느껴지지 않는 손색없는 번역으로 인정받았다. 이 시리즈는 세계인들에게 문학 한류의 지속적인 힘과 가능성을 입증하는 전집이 될 것이다.

바이링궐 에디션 한국 대표 소설 set 1

분단 Division

01 병신과 머저리-**이청준** The Wounded-**Yi Cheong-jun**
02 어둠의 혼-**김원일** Soul of Darkness-**Kim Won-il**
03 순이삼촌-**현기영** Sun-i Samch'on-**Hyun Ki-young**
04 엄마의 말뚝 1-**박완서** Mother's Stake I-**Park Wan-suh**
05 유형의 땅-**조정래** The Land of the Banished-**Jo Jung-rae**

산업화 Industrialization

06 무진기행-**김승옥** Record of a Journey to Mujin-**Kim Seung-ok**
07 삼포 가는 길-**황석영** The Road to Sampo-**Hwang Sok-yong**
08 아홉 켤레의 구두로 남은 사내-**윤흥길** The Man Who Was Left as Nine Pairs of Shoes-**Yun Heung-gil**
09 돌아온 우리의 친구-**신상웅** Our Friend's Homecoming-**Shin Sang-ung**
10 원미동 시인-**양귀자** The Poet of Wŏnmi-dong-**Yang Kwi-ja**

여성 Women

11 중국인 거리-**오정희** Chinatown-**Oh Jung-hee**
12 풍금이 있던 자리-**신경숙** The Place Where the Harmonium Was-**Shin Kyung-sook**
13 하나코는 없다-**최윤** The Last of Hanak'o-**Ch'oe Yun**
14 인간에 대한 예의-**공지영** Human Decency-**Gong Ji-young**
15 빈처-**은희경** Poor Man's Wife-**Eun Hee-kyung**

바이링궐 에디션 한국 대표 소설 set 2

자유 Liberty

16 필론의 돼지-**이문열** Pilon's Pig-**Yi Mun-yol**
17 슬로우 불릿-**이대환** Slow Bullet-**Lee Dae-hwan**
18 직선과 독가스-**임철우** Straight Lines and Poison Gas-**Lim Chul-woo**
19 깃발-**홍희담** The Flag-**Hong Hee-dam**
20 새벽 출정-**방현석** Off to Battle at Dawn-**Bang Hyeon-seok**

사랑과 연애 Love and Love Affairs

21 별을 사랑하는 마음으로-**윤후명** With the Love for the Stars-**Yun Hu-myong**
22 목련공원-**이승우** Magnolia Park-**Lee Seung-u**
23 칼에 찔린 자국-**김인숙** Stab-**Kim In-suk**
24 회복하는 인간-**한강** Convalescence-**Han Kang**
25 트렁크-**정이현** In the Trunk-**Jeong Yi-hyun**

남과 북 South and North

26 판문점-**이호철** Panmunjom-**Yi Ho-chol**
27 수난 이대-**하근찬** The Suffering of Two Generations-**Ha Geun-chan**
28 분지-**남정현** Land of Excrement-**Nam Jung-hyun**
29 봄 실상사-**정도상** Spring at Silsangsa Temple-**Jeong Do-sang**
30 은행나무 사랑-**김하기** Gingko Love-**Kim Ha-kee**

바이링궐 에디션 한국 대표 소설 set 3

서울 Seoul

31 눈사람 속의 검은 항아리-**김소진** The Dark Jar within the Snowman-**Kim So-jin**
32 오후, 가로지르다-**하성란** Traversing Afternoon-**Ha Seong-nan**
33 나는 봉천동에 산다-**조경란** I Live in Bongcheon-dong-**Jo Kyung-ran**
34 그렇습니까? 기린입니다-**박민규** Is That So? I'm A Giraffe-**Park Min-gyu**
35 성탄특선-**김애란** Christmas Specials-**Kim Ae-ran**

전통 Tradition

36 무자년의 가을 사흘-**서정인** Three Days of Autumn, 1948-**Su Jung-in**
37 유자소전-**이문구** A Brief Biography of Yuja-**Yi Mun-gu**
38 향기로운 우물 이야기-**박범신** The Fragrant Well-**Park Bum-shin**
39 월행-**송기원** A Journey under the Moonlight-**Song Ki-won**
40 협죽도 그늘 아래-**성석제** In the Shade of the Oleander-**Song Sok-ze**

아방가르드 Avant-garde

41 아겔다마-**박상륭** Akeldama-**Park Sang-ryoong**
42 내 영혼의 우물-**최인석** A Well in My Soul-**Choi In-seok**
43 당신에 대해서-**이인성** On You-**Yi In-seong**
44 회색 時-**배수아** Time In Gray-**Bae Su-ah**
45 브라운 부인-**정영문** Mrs. Brown-**Jung Young-moon**

바이링궐 에디션 한국 대표 소설 set 4

디아스포라 Diaspora

46 속옷-**김남일** Underwear-**Kim Nam-il**
47 상하이에 두고 온 사람들-**공선옥** People I Left in Shanghai-**Gong Sun-ok**
48 모두에게 복된 새해-**김연수** Happy New Year to Everyone-**Kim Yeon-su**
49 코끼리-**김재영** The Elephant-**Kim Jae-young**
50 먼지별-**이경** Dust Star-**Lee Kyung**

가족 Family

51 혜자의 눈꽃-**천승세** Hye-ja's Snow-Flowers-**Chun Seung-sei**
52 아베의 가족-**전상국** Ahbe's Family-**Jeon Sang-guk**
53 문 앞에서-**이동하** Outside the Door-**Lee Dong-ha**
54 그리고, 축제-**이혜경** And Then the Festival-**Lee Hye-kyung**
55 봄밤-**권여선** Spring Night-**Kwon Yeo-sun**

유머 Humor

56 오늘의 운세-**한창훈** Today's Fortune-**Han Chang-hoon**
57 새-**전성태** Bird-**Jeon Sung-tae**
58 밀수록 다시 가까워지는-**이기호** So Far, and Yet So Near-**Lee Ki-ho**
59 유리방패-**김중혁** The Glass Shield-**Kim Jung-hyuk**
60 전당포를 찾아서-**김종광** The Pawnshop Chase-**Kim Chong-kwang**